Also by Brenda Hasse

On The Third Day

~

Brenda Hasse

On The Third Day

ISBN: 978-0-9906312-2-4 (pbk)

ISBN: 978-0-9906312-3-1 (ebk)

Printed in the United States of America

To Sheila,

Message received.

For the dearly departed,

May our Lord greet them with open arms upon their arrival home and bring comfort to those they have left behind.

Dear Reader,

You open your eyes to darkness and place your hand upon your chest verifying the rapid beat of your heart. It takes a moment for you to orientate yourself. After wiping the sweat from your brow and taking a few deep breaths, you realize you are in your bedroom lying in bed. Brushing away the tears from your cheeks, you flip your pillow over to avoid resting your face on the dampness as you roll onto your side, close your eyes, and hope to return to sleep, but haunting details of the dream begin to replay within your mind. They are vivid and lifelike, as if you were an actor portraying a character in a play or sitting in the audience watching a performance. Knowing sleep is futile, you open your eyes and begin to analyze its possible meaning.

Dreams are diverse. Their details may include a deceased relative or friend, a possible prediction of something that may happen in the future, or difficult to understand with strange hodgepodge objects and nonsensical happenings.

Some dreams shake you to your core, strike fear within your soul, and hauntingly replay within your mind. You may wonder if there was a specific message the person tried to convey. Is it possible to receive messages from those who reside in the spiritual world? Can they communicate to us through our dreams?

When we dream during twilight, the moment between awake and asleep, we can recall most of the details upon awakening. Some people believe that those in the nonphysical world can utilize dreams to communicate with us during this opportune time. Maybe a passed loved one chose to convey their message through the representation of something they were fond of when they were alive, such as a dragonfly or a fairy, or use a barrier such as a fogged window to allow us to see them only as a mere shadow. Others may use words or colors within the projected pictures. Whatever their vice, their visitation had a purpose, and their message was significant.

It is common to confide and share your dream with someone, especially if it was upsetting. It may be helpful to listen to their interpretation and how they view it from a different perspective.

Dreams have been shared and recorded throughout history. Even the Bible refers to them as visions or dreams and mentions them occurring nearly one hundred times. Does this suggest that God or angels may use dreams to convey their messages too?

On The Third Day is a diary of the messages I have received either in the form of a dream or as a picture flashed within my mind. Sometimes the message is easy to understand, and I can recognize the person conveying it. Other times, the message is vague, and I assume the meaning will be revealed when needed. Some of the messages are intended for others and I relay the information to the individual.

After a friend or family member passes away and if they choose to visit me through a dream, they usually will do so by the third day following their death. A line in the Apostle's Creed states, 'on the third day he rose from the dead'. Is this a coincidence? Just as Jesus did, do we each have three days after our death before we cross over to the other side?

On occasion those who have communicated with me may have more than one message and will continue to visit me through dreams and visions until they know they have been understood.

Even though the main character of this book is fictional, the dreams she invokes are messages I have received. I hope to make others aware of the significance of their dreams and encourage everyone to give credence to the possible messages within them.

It was important for the messenger to communicate through a dream or vision. Perhaps it would be wise to listen.

Sincerely,
Brenda Hasse
Author

My Death

My mother's eyes, so full of pride, my hands gripping my father's strong index finger as I take my first step, blowing out birthday candles, waving good-bye to my father as I turn and walk alone through the open double doors on my first day of school, remembering the magic of adding two numbers together and calculating the answer, blurred years of endless classrooms and teachers, difficulty learning to read, homework, playing with our family dog, rescuing our adopted cat, the many dance classes, costumes, and recitals, childhood friends, college roommates, my first real job, walking down the aisle of the church to commit my life to the man I love, the first time I held each of my children in my arms and inhaled their sweet fragrance, helping them with their homework, making food for them to eat, watching them open Christmas presents, laughing at their excitement when they found the Easter eggs and their baskets, helping the children learn to ride a bike and crossing my fingers in hope that they would remain upright, beaming with pride at their report card grades, attending their sporting events as their most loyal fan, cringing with each fall and cheering as they rose, my business and the dedicated work to make it a successful entity in the community and a legacy for my children…the happiness, the sadness, the good times, the bad times, the love, so much love…it all flashed before my eyes.

I don't remember being born, but this, this dying I would remember. It seemed quite easy as I expelled my last breath, my heart stilled, and I surrendered my existence in this world.

How many times had I prayed to God to not take me away from my family? I was too young to die, or at least I thought so. I wondered why my eventual departure from them involved a long, drawn out illness with endless doctor visits, testing, medical procedures, pain, and suffering. It would have been less of a strain on my family if I would have perished in a fatal car accident or died from a heart attack. Maybe my prolonged battle with cancer was a subtle way of pushing me toward the acceptance of my death.

I opened my eyes. Gone was the pain, the struggle to breathe as my weightless body began to float upward toward the tiles of the drop ceiling.

"*Fear not.*" A kind voice spoke.

My eyes widened at the unexpected words reverberating within the room.

In the final months of my life, my doctors had taken an aggressive approach to fight my cancer. The combination of chemotherapy and antibiotics resulted in the loss of my hearing. Had my ears deceived me?

I remained perfectly still as if paralyzed and listened intently while the tiny holes in the ceiling tiles drew closer to my face. An annoying hum echoing within the room penetrated my ears. Did I also hear crying? It was behind me, or should I say beneath me? I twisted and rotated in the air toward the floor and saw my body lying in a hospital bed. The machine adjacent to it displayed a flat green line. My husband sat in a chair with my hand clasped gently within his. He wiped a tear from his cheek before exhaling deeply and looking to the children, who were standing beside my bed with their eyes cast downward toward my still body.

"It's over." He stood and kissed my forehead.

In a way he seemed relieved. I couldn't blame him. Gone was the worrying, the chaotic family schedule, and the endless trips to the hospital to spend time with me during my final days. I hoped he thought he had done all he could to see me through to the end of my life. I prayed he didn't feel guilty to still be alive or wished he could have done more for me. In time I hoped he realized he had done his best to support me through to the end. Now, he had to continue without me and move forward with his life. It is what I wanted for him most of all.

My daughter dabbed a tissue to each cheek and blotted her eyes. My son, not quite sure of how to act, glanced at her sideways as if afraid of invading her privacy. In the end, he put his arm around her shoulders.

"She's gone," my husband placed my arm to the side of my body and patted my hand, "and at peace."

Some may wonder why I chose to take my final breath in a hospital room. I knew I would be more comfortable dying at home, but my reason is an unselfish one. I didn't want my family to continue to reside in a house where I had died. Heaven forbid they superstitiously believe my spirit still resided within its walls. Even though the idea may offer them comfort, it would be difficult to part with the house if and when they choose to sell it.

My husband attempted a smile as he turned toward the children. Even though my daughter would be entering her last year in high school, it was comforting to see her step into his opened arms and accept the comfort that he offered. My son stood nearby timidly. He was at that awkwardly stage of being old enough to be treated like an adult, yet young enough to still be a child at heart. He scratched the peach fuzz on his chin as he tilted his face toward the ceiling trying to disguise the tears welling in his eyes. *Yes, tough men do cry, my dear.* It is a lesson he would learn, and perhaps now was the time to do so.

My husband reached over and clasped his shoulder encouraging our son to be drawn into his embrace, and he complied. He hugged them closely to his chest as if attempting to give them strength and absorb their grief. As if afraid he would give into his personal loss, he stared at the wall silently while trying to control his quivering bottom lip. Loosening his embrace, he looked down into their reddened eyes and smiled slightly to reassure them.

"We'll be fine. We'll be fine."

After my world had grown silent, it was reassuring to hear my husband's strong and confident voice once again. I remember the first time I heard it.

I was attending a fraternity party with my college roommate. A deep, resonant laugh from across the room drew my attention. He was tall, very tall. I assumed his major differed from mine, for I had not noticed him in any of my classes. After being drawn back into my roommate's conversation, a commanding, but gentle voice resonated from behind me.

"So, how are you doing in Econ?"

As I turned around, I found myself staring at a sweatshirt logo before looking up into his chestnut eyes.

"I'm sorry, but how do you know I have Econ?"

"I sit in the back of the auditorium. You usually arrive after I do and sit seven rows ahead and three seats to the left of me." The deep tone of his voice was calm and comforting and contradicted his intimidating height and size, a true gentle giant. I was impressed. As if the classroom was a piece of grid paper, he had taken the time to count the rows and seats to determine my exact location.

That was our beginning. We dated through college and married upon graduation. Once our children were born, he would cradle them in his large hands and speak softly to soothe them when they were cranky and colicky. They usually quieted quickly as they became wide eyed in recognition of his voice, stared into his face, and listened intently. Sometimes they would coo or screech in an attempt to explain their ailment to him. He would respond kindly as if he understood their gibberish.

As I looked down upon them, I knew my husband's strength would see them through this difficult time.

"*You may come down.*"

My husband had not spoken. It was someone else's voice, but who? I looked at the corner of the room to see a man, or at least I thought it was a man. He was dressed in a luminescent white robe that appeared as soft as an angora sweater. His face radiated kindness.

"Did you say something?"

He nodded his head in affirmation.

I twisted and turned in the air to descend. Apparently, gravity is no longer an issue. With frustration setting in, I stopped struggling and stared at the stranger.

"How do I come down to the floor?"

"*Imagine it and it shall be.*"

His lips did not move, yet I heard his voice within my mind. *He communicates telepathically*, I thought. I was confused.

"Yes."

I heard his reply to my unspoken assumption. I looked at the floor but did not descend.

"Picture it within your mind."

I closed my eyes and imagined myself standing on the floor next to my family. Opening my eyes, I had relocated to where I had envisioned.

"Can they see me?" I waved the palm of my hand before my husband's face. He did not react.

"No."

Turning toward the man, I stood firmly in place as he took a step toward me.

"Who are you?"

"I am your spirit guide."

"My what?"

"Some refer to me as a guardian angel."

"I thought only children have guardian angels."

"I have been with you from the moment a tiny spark of light indicated your conception until now, and I will remain by your side in the afterlife until deemed unnecessary."

"Oh, my G…goodness, if you were always there then you saw me naked while I showered and while my husband and I had sex."

"Do not feel ashamed, for you chose your body type. You are perfect, even though you believe you are not. As far as your

relationship with your husband, it is natural and enabled the birth of your children."

"And you watched us?"

"I stood nearby, guarding, as always."

"Guarding?"

"Yes, it is my purpose. I have also instilled ideas, invoked your imagination, and stirred your consciousness when necessary."

My daughter turned away from my husband and looked toward my body.

"What do we do now?"

Her inquiry drew my attention as my husband replied.

"We wait. Someone should come into the room soon."

"I'm dead." It was more of a statement than a question.

"Yes, you have fulfilled this life's purpose."

Knowing her question was misunderstood, my daughter clarified.

"That's not what I meant."

The rapid footsteps echoing from the hallway grew louder as if broadcasting the nurses' arrival to the room. Unable to avoid the collision, my eyes enlarged apprehensively as I stepped backward just before the woman passed through me. I turned to see my family move aside as she went to the monitor. I peeked over her shoulder as she looked at the glowing green line, clasped my wrist, and felt for a pulse. Removing the stethoscope from around her neck, she listened to my chest before turning to my family.

"I'm sorry for your loss." Her comment had been well rehearsed. Perhaps it was her way of staying unattached to the family's grief.

"Thank you." My husband acknowledged.

Several clicks resonated as the nurse shut off the various machines until the flat green line on the monitor disappeared, the incessant hum ceased, and the digital readout blackened confirming the end of my life.

Displaying a polite nod of condolence to the children, the nurse redirected her attention to my husband.

"I assume you have made arrangements."

"Yes, well, she did. I believe it is in her paperwork." He confirmed.

"Thank you. I will check her chart." The nurse left the room.

"You didn't answer my question, Dad." My daughter continued.

At the sound of her sincere statement, my husband redirected his attention toward her.

"What do we do now?"

"We do as Mom planned."

You mean the way 'we' planned, dear.

As my illness progressed and my body weakened, we were forced to face the reality of my impending death. I remember the day my husband came into our bedroom, and we began planning for the future he would face without me by his side. I knew he would go through many stages of grief, experience loneliness, and degrees of depression. It could not be helped, but it was important he proceed with life as normally as possible, even though there would be nothing normal about it. We both cried throughout the conversation and those that followed to discuss each topic methodically. Much of what we talked about was written down. Some of it was not. I hoped he could recall all we had discussed. At times when I was alone, I would review each aspect in detail by committing to pen and paper everything taken into consideration and other topics we had forgotten. I had left explicit details for my funeral, personal items, and business, for I didn't want him to be burdened with trying to guess what I would have wanted. It was my final gift, a way of making things easier for him and the children.

They stood in the silence of the private room and stared at my lifeless body. My daughter exhaled before wiping a tear away from her cheek.

My son broke his silence.

"I'm glad Mom is at peace, but I miss her already. I mean, even though she really wasn't with us toward the end, in a way she was physically. I always hoped she would get well, but now that she's dead, what hope I had for her recovery has died with her."

"My son, the poetic voice of reason." I smiled. *Such a mature point of view coming from someone so young.* He had grown weary of my suffering and seemed relieved. It couldn't have been easy for him to watch me die. I couldn't blame him for feeling so.

I had battled my illness for several years. I knew it was stressful for him, for all of them, but I could do nothing more than put up a good fight until my time came. I had to agree with his analysis. Accepting my death meant also accepting that all hope was lost.

"At least she is no longer in pain." My daughter looked at my peaceful face.

Spoken like an adult. God, I love them so very much. My heart swelled with pride. I know this moment was difficult for them to face, but such is life. We live, we die. Maybe the purpose of my illness was to foreshadow my death and help them cope with it more easily. At least their lives would resume some sort of normalcy. No more doctor visits resulting in bad news. No more vigils at my bedroom ensuring I was comfortable. No more driving to and from the hospital. I hoped they would soon put this experience behind them, remember the good times with fondness, and move forward with their lives.

I went to the side of the bed and examined my lifeless body. Other than the failure of my chest rising and falling, one would assume I was sleeping. I cringed at the sight of my invisible eyelashes. Before my illness, it was my habit to apply my make-up daily and dare not leave home without it on. There were too many within the community who knew me. I never knew who I may run into at the grocery store or post office. Oh, how I wish I had mascara on them now. I know it may be silly and a little shallow, but it would have been nice for my family to remember me looking my best.

My body was wearing the lovely hospital gown with the air conditioning in the back. It really didn't matter. I was never one for the latest fashion. In fact, I hated shopping. I thought it was a waste of time. However, it would have been nice to die in my cozy, ratty pajamas with the three-corner tear in the left thigh of my pant leg and a missing button on the top. I assume my family thought they were a little too embarrassing for me to wear in the hospital or the nursing staff insisted that I was dressed in their functional gown.

My attention was drawn to a rectangle of light upon the floor. I glanced out the window to the beam of sunshine cresting the edge of a cloud. It was morning, perhaps near midday. My family looked tired. They had stayed with me through the night knowing my time was drawing near. It was comforting to know they were with me even though they may have assumed I was unaware of their presence.

"They look exhausted. God bless them."

"*He does.*"

I took a step toward my spirit guide.

"Since I'm dead, why do I need you to watch over me any longer?"

"*I am here for your protection during your journey home.*"

"Protect me from what exactly?"

"*From those who collect souls.*"

"I assume the soul collectors are bad?"

"*Very much so. He has asked me to guide you safely home.*"

"He?"

"*Yes, and I shall do so as He has requested. Are you ready to begin our journey?*"

I stared at my family's sullen faces. The thought of separating from them caused a pang within my heart. I felt cheated, cheated by the shortness of my life. I would be absent from my children's future milestones, unavailable when they sought advise during a difficult time, and my place in the church pew would be vacant during their marriage ceremony. I would never hold my grandchildren in my arms and hear 'grandma' uttered from their precious lips.

"*You will be there but remain unseen.*" My guide interrupted my thoughts.

I turned toward him, a little angered by his comment.

"But I want to be there, physically, and have them see me too. That's what a mom is supposed to do."

"*Your purposed has been fulfilled. You have accomplished what you were supposed to do, and you have done it well. It is time for you to return home.*"

"I don't want to go yet. I want to make sure they will be fine without me."

"*It is a common response.*"

"More than anything, I want to tell them that I love them and say good-bye. I didn't get to say good-bye." I didn't have many regrets in life, but this was one of them.

"*I shall stay with you, but as He was given the time, so shall you have until the third day to prepare for the journey.*"

"Third day?"

"*Yes, as you have recited the prayer many times before 'on the third day...'*"

The words registered within my mind as I completed the sentence.

"He rose again."

"*Yes, as shall you.*"

"Good-bye Mom." My son placed his hand upon my lifeless one and brushed away the tears rolling down his cheeks. I stepped next to him and put my hand on his arm, but it passed through it. How I wished to comfort him.

He looked at his shoulder and brushed his hand across it. Could he have felt my touch?

"It felt as if there was a spider on my shoulder." He explained as he looked at his father.

Sighing despairingly, I bowed my head. I wished I could hold him in my arms one last time. He continued.

"Even though I know your love will remain within my heart, I will miss you, but never forget you. It eases my mind to know you are no longer in pain." He released my hand and stepped away to allow his sister to approach the bed.

"Bye Mom." My daughter looked at my face. "I love you, but you already know that." She patted my hand before turning and joining her brother.

"Yes, I know." I whispered to myself as I watched my children step through the doorway and into the hallway. I looked back toward the love of my life standing alone in the room. He exhaled deeply before placing his hand upon mine and drawing his face closely to my face as if I could hear what he needed to say. Little did he know, I could.

"In a way, I'm relieved because I know you are in a better place. I can usually fix almost anything, but I couldn't fix this. I felt helpless watching you suffer, knowing there was nothing I could do to make it better." His eyes welled with tears expressing his frustration. "I will never forget the day we met at college." He began to reminisce. "I am thankful for the time we had together and cherish each and every day. You are my first love, my one and only. I can't imagine how I am going to go on without you, but in truth, I have little choice. I will do my best to raise our children as we have discussed. I'm not perfect, so don't laugh at me when I make mistakes. I hope, somehow, you will guide me through the tough decisions I might face. I promise to make sure the children have a Christmas filled with as much happiness as possible. You know I love you with all of my heart and always will."

"I love you too." I wanted to touch him one last time, to kiss him on the cheek, wrap my arms around him, and promise him that everything would be all right. Unfortunately, the promise would be false. I didn't know what lay ahead in his future.

Pulling the sheet gently from beneath my arms, he lifted it over my head, wiped the tears from his cheeks, and joined the children in the hall.

My shrouded body would be taken to the hospital mortuary until the funeral director collected it. I had expected my husband's train of thought to be clouded by grief, so I relieved him from the responsibility of arranging my funeral. I ensured my final arrangements were secure before my health had deteriorated to unconsciousness.

My funeral included a simple service at our church with a burial to follow. The clothing for my service was at the funeral home. The organist knew my choice of music. The secretary at the church knew the scripture readings for the Mass. I had updated the family will through our lawyer. It entitled my husband to all my assets, including ownership of my small press publishing partnership. There were a few personal things I gave the children, mostly jewelry. It was comforting to know I had most of my final wishes addressed, at least all of the ones that were most dear to me.

I looked toward my guide.

"Now what?"

"*You indicated a desire to remain, ensure others will continue without you, and say farewell. Who do you wish to visit first?*"

"I only have three days?"

"*Yes.*"

"If the people I want to visit can't see or hear me, how do I say good-bye to them?"

"*Through their dreams.*"

Through their dreams? I tried to comprehend his meaning. *Through their dreams.*

"Do you mean while they are sleeping?"

"*Yes.*"

"But they only sleep at night. That isn't three days. It's three nights." I argued with the hope of justifying the need for more time. "How am I to visit those dearest to me in so little time?"

"*It is the time allowed.*"

I was dumbfounded, my mind racing. *Think.* I was used to deadlines. *On the third day.* There were many friends, business associates, and family I wished to visit one last time, but the constraint of saying farewell while they slept reduced my options drastically. I would have to prioritize.

I had the feeling I may want to visit with my son, daughter, and husband more than once. Even though I knew I had left them physically, it gave me a sense of relief to know I would be near them for the next few days. I hoped they knew I loved them. In fact, I knew they did, but there was a need within me to ensure they understood the magnitude of the love I held for them within my heart.

I needed to organize my thoughts. *What hasn't been said? What do I wanted to tell them?* I must choose each message carefully to ensure it conveys what I want them to know without misunderstanding or misinterpretation. Echoing voices in the hallway drew my attention. I watched two nurses pass by the doorway before I spoke to my spirit guide beside me.

"Since I have to wait until they are sleeping, I believe I would like to visit a few of my favorite places."

"*Very well. Imagine it and it shall be.*"

I closed my eyes and pictured the first place, a place of joy and happy memories with my children.

Day 1

My Favorite Places

I stood in the center of the city park. The grass was mowed and tidy. The flowerboxes with their vibrant pink, orange, and white foliage decorated the railing of the gazebo, the symbol of our small city.

"I spent a lot of time here with my children."

"*Yes, I know.*"

It was bittersweet to recall our traditional end of the elementary school year celebration. After picking them up from their last day of school, we would stop at our local candy store, purchase a little brown paper surprise bag of candy, and walk across the street to the park located in the heart of downtown. My children eagerly climbed the few steps of the gazebo, sat on the floor, and opened their bags to view its contents. Unable to contain his excitement, my son often emptied his entire bag onto the wooden floor. They would choose a piece of candy and stuff it into their mouth, return the remaining pieces to their brown bag, and give them to me to hold while they went to the swing set to play.

I watched as two children ran past me, selected a swing, and kicked their legs upward to the sky in an attempt to outdo each other. A little boy sat in the brown plastic chair swing while a woman pushed him forward gently. The swing set had been updated since my children played on them years ago. It was nice to see the improvement. Sometimes change is a good thing, especially when there has been an improvement in safety.

I turned toward the babbling water of the dam and its churning stream below. An elderly couple sat upon a bench at the river's edge mesmerized by the water rippling over the dam. It saddened me a little. I had pictured my husband and I doing the same one day.

A squeal of excitement caused me to turn and see a little girl reeling in a small bluegill. The fish wiggled and danced at the end of her line as she placed it upon the ground.

I remember my children having the same reaction to the fish they would catch from the river during their summer months. When the children wanted to go fishing, their job was to dig up the worms. My job was to bait their hooks. They would cast their lines and wait patiently for a fish to latch onto it. I would don my garden gloves as they let out a cheerful glee and began to reel in their catch. The gloves protected my hands from the dorsal fin. No need to tempt fate, safety first. Most of the fish were tiny and easy to remove from the hook, but the larger ones often swallowed it. With my needle nose pliers in hand, I would meticulously withdraw the hook causing as little damage to the fish as possible. We never kept their catch. In truth, I didn't want to clean them. Fishing was my way of teaching my children patience, but releasing their catch also taught them compassion and to respect life.

A stout, gray haired woman sat alone on a bench near the river's edge. She reached into a plastic bag, took out a stale slice of bread, and broke it into pieces. She tossed bits of bread to the cluster of ducks floating nearby in the water.

A little girl with blonde pigtails pulled on her mother's hand and approached the elderly woman. She studied her movements as she tossed the pieces of bread into the water and smiled as the ducks darted and ate the soggy bits with their beaks. She looked back to the old woman, who smiled and patted the seat next to her.

"Thank you." The young woman lifted her daughter onto the bench and sat next to her.

The elderly woman reached into the plastic bag, withdrew a slice of bread, and handed half of it to the little girl before explaining how to tear it pieces. The little girl watched before imitating.

I turned toward a clattering of metal behind me and watched as my guide's height increased until he became nearly eight feet tall or more. His robe shortened to mid-thigh revealing leather boots laced to his knees and muscular legs. His chest was protected by a sleeveless armor plate made of brass. He resembled a Roman warrior. Majestic golden feathered wings emerged and unfolded from his back. The scraping of metal against metal resonated as he pulled his sword from its sheath and held the long blade upward as if readying for battle. He turned his head as if listening for the slightest sound.

"Oh my." I took a step backward to appreciate his full height, but he stopped my retreat by encircling my body within his protective wings and drawing me near him.

"*There is danger. We must move on.*"

I turned my back to him, peeked through the feathers of his wing, and glanced around the park, but saw nothing out of the ordinary.

"Soul collectors? Where?"

"*I have called upon others to help, but we must move to another location now.*"

His voice reverberated within my mind. It was insistent, tinged with panic. I looked at the sky expecting to see angels or archangels descending from Heaven but saw nothing.

"Very well." Closing my eyes, I imagined the next place I wanted to visit.

His wings retracted like an opening curtain on a stage as I inhaled the aroma of chocolate. Our town prided itself in having our very own candy maker. The quaint little shop's showcases were filled with handmade chocolates, truffles, and various flavors of chocolate bark. Another showcase contained popular candy carried in most grocery stores. Behind the counter was a basket filled with the brown paper surprise bags, a very popular item since it could be purchased for a quarter or two. The opposite wall contained large jars of jellybeans, mints, and other candy of every kind imaginable that could be purchased by the pound. The owner also carried many gift items for special occasions.

I peered over my shoulder and then upward as my guardian rotated his sword and returned it to its sheath. His wings folded toward his back, and he resumed his normal height and clothing.

"Very impressive."

"*It was necessary.*"

"Thank you." I was unaware of the severity of the situation, but grateful that my guide was there for my protection.

"*You are welcome.*" He bowed his head respectfully as if pleased to be of service.

The employees of the quaint shop were busy helping customers. The clerk behind the counter retrieved various chocolates as requested by a woman and filled a small white box, another handed a small surprise bag to a little girl as her mother paid for the treat, and another assisted an elderly woman who was too short to reach an item on a top shelf. More than likely, it was a gift she was purchasing for someone.

"Out of all of the candy in this store, my children enjoyed the surprise bags the most. They have gone up in price since we purchased them years ago." I explained to my guide, who remained silent.

I stepped closer to examine the handmade chocolates in the display cases. They were various shapes, sizes, and colors; dark, milk, or white chocolate. Some were decorated with a candy flower or drizzled of contrasting chocolate. *Chocolate, my favorite food group.*

"I think I enjoyed dark chocolate the best." I admitted as I glanced behind me to see my guide peering out the front display window. He remained vigilant, scanning the park, street, and sky. Certain he could hear me, I continued.

"I could never understand the quote by Forrest Gump. 'Life is like a box of chocolates. You never know what you're gonna get.' His box of chocolates looked like the kind you can purchase from a grocery store. All he had to do was look on the underside of the lid where he would find a printed diagram of each chocolate and its flavor." I smiled at my silly analogy, but the quote wouldn't apply to these boxes of chocolates. Each one is different based on the customer's preference. "There's nothing like the small town feel of genuine customer service."

I wondered if there was chocolate or if I would need to eat once we were 'home.' I inhaled the aroma one final time and looked at my guide.

"Is it safe for us to go to the next stop?"

"*Yes.*"

"It isn't very far. Just two doors down." I closed my eyes and imagining the next shop I wanted to visit.

I opened my eyes to see shelves of books. Ah, the bookstore, my favorite escape from reality. Best sellers and new titles on the shelf to my left were always an interest of mine. Oh, and historical romance, a must have on a cold and rainy day. However, one could never go wrong with a classic. I had to admit, Jane Austen's novels were a favorite of mine. Her insight into the different way each protagonist fell in love is ingenious, especially considering her background and the time period in which she lived. I can't recall the number of times I read *Pride and Prejudice*. Ah, Mr. Darcy. I believe I read Persuasion and Sense and Sensibility a few times as well.

The smoke from a fragrant pipe filled the air. I peeked over a bookcase to see a gentleman standing in the front corner of the store. He was wearing a mid-thigh length brown and beige tweed jacket and pants with a white shirt. His neck was donned with a dark brown bow tie. Atop his head was a brown and beige plaid deerstalker hat. His vest was made of the same material as his hat. With a pipe pinched between his lips, he reminded me of Sherlock Holmes. His left hand held a walking stick. He came around the end of the bookshelf and stood in the aisle before me. He removed the pipe from his mouth and tipped his hat.

"It is a pleasure to make your acquaintance." He clasped my hand within his, kissed its back, and released it before standing erect.

"It is a pleasure to meet you as well." I looked at his brown leather shoes donned with light brown spats. I believe the style was popular during the end of the Victorian period, maybe later. He appeared to be a true gentleman. I looked at his walking stick.

He followed my line of sight.

"It was a gift." He held it before me, and I examined the brass lion head handle.

"It's beautiful."

"Thank you." He returned the walking stick to the floor with a tap and rested his hand upon it. "I have seen you in the bookstore before. You were here frequently."

"Yes. Reading is a pleasure of mine."

"Mine as well. Or it was." He took a handkerchief from his pants pocket and stared at the embroidered initial. "I do apologize for not introducing myself, but I can't quite remember my name. I assume it began with an 'H', but I am uncertain if it represents my first name or my last." He held the monogrammed handkerchief before me to examine, as if to prove his point.

The 'H' was beautifully embroidered with delicate stitches. I wondered if his wife had made it or perhaps, he had received it as a gift too.

"It's lovely." I examined the intricate stitches. "I believe it is the first letter in your last name, or at least that is protocol in monogramming an article of clothing."

He gave it an approving glance before returning it to his pocket.

"I do remember my name. It's Marie Michaels."

"A lovely name for a lovely lady."

"Thank you." I smiled at the compliment and looked at his eyes. They were kind. By my estimation, he was in his mid-60s, maybe a little older.

"You are a resident here." It wasn't a question. I knew the answer.

"Yes, for an eternity it seems. I used to live across town when I was alive."

A lost soul.

"From your style of clothing, which is very nice I may add, you have been here many years."

He looked at his clothing and then to mine.

"In my day, I drove a horse and carriage, not these horseless carriages I see out the window today." He motioned with his pipe toward the store window where books were displayed to draw in window shoppers.

If I recalled my history correctly, Henry Ford produced his first automobile in 1903, but it must have been a few years before it became a popular mode of transportation. I knew our city was established in 1834, but his clothing indicated he lived between 1890 to 1920, at least that's when spats were popular.

He knocked a book off the shelf and watched it fall before looking up at me with a devilish smirk.

"I like to let them know I am here." He chuckled.

We watched as the middle-aged woman walked to the fallen book, picked it up, and looked around the store.

"Jack, be nice." She warned as she placed the book in its proper spot on the shelf.

"She calls me Jack." He conveyed with a bit of pride in his voice.

"Can she see you?" I inquired.

"No, but at least she acknowledges that I'm here. One employee can see me, but she isn't working today."

"So, it was you who knocked off a book or two during my visits?"

His smiled and admitted his guilt with a nod of his head.

"I had mentioned the incident to one of the women. She said they knew they had a spirit in the store that liked to cause mischief such as items falling from the shelves or books turned around so their spines faced the back of the shelf."

He exhaled pipe smoke in the direction of the employee as she walked past him. She wrinkled her nose and waved her hand before her face to dissipate the strong order.

"Oh, I remember smelling the fragrance of your pipe, but I assumed it was the elderly man from the jewelry store. He would smoke his pipe while he walked up and down the street during his break."

He looked at my guide. "I see you didn't arrive through the portal."

"The portal? What portal?" I looked at the floor in fear that I may step in it and fall down to who knows where.

"On the wall, where the plaster is missing." He pointed above the bookshelves near the back of the store.

I turned to see the exposed brick. "The portal is there? I only see brick."

"Ah, then you have recently passed."

"Yes, earlier today."

"*Only lost souls are able to use the portals.*" My guide explained as he stood near me.

With my curiosity piqued, I looked back to H.

"Where does it go?"

"I don't know. I have never used it."

"It appears you have been in the store for quite some time."

"I believe I once owned a business here, but I'm not sure anymore." He became lost in thought for a moment as he looked around the store. "I think I owned a hardware store."

"But aren't you curious to find out where it leads, perhaps go to other places?"

"No. I watch others come and go through it. They share amazing tales of their lives and the time in which they lived.

Others remember very little. Where it leads, I do not care. I decided long ago that I like it here and here is where I shall stay."

The click of switches echoed throughout the small store. The lights went dark except for one left on for security.

"If you will excuse me, madam, I like to sit in the window and watch those who pass by the shop on their way to dinner. Would you care to join me?"

"No, thank you." I looked out the display window to notice the sun disappear behind the tops of the trees. "It was nice meeting you, sir."

"It has been a pleasure meeting you as well. Good luck on your journey forward." He tipped his hat, went to the window, and floated to the top left corner near the adjacent brick wall. I assumed the elevated height gave him the advantage of viewing the comings and goings on the street.

I looked around the small bookstore one last time. It was quaint, the kind of shop with a small-town appeal. Its rows filled with pages of adventures, knowledge, and other worlds for patrons to purchase and enjoy. I sighed.

"Perhaps we should be on our way." I suggested to my guide.

I passed through the front door with my guide in tow. Pausing on the sidewalk, I looked at the top of the bookstore window and waved to H. He removed the pipe from his mouth and nodded his head in acknowledgement.

The city's improvement committee recently installed old fashioned style streetlamps to complement our historic community. They illuminated our way as we toured the main street, which was a favorite pastime of mine during my lunch hour. On a nice summer day, I would stretch my legs with a walk to the park, purchase an ice cream cone, and window shop the small businesses.

A young couple walking arm in arm crossed the street at the intersection and turned toward us. The gentleman tipped his black Derby hat and the woman smiled in acknowledgement before passing by me and continuing their conversation. Their clothing was old, very old. Her hooped skirt looked like a bell swaying with each step. A satin ribbon tied beneath her chin secured her straw bonnet atop of her head. With her arm entwined within his, they appeared in love. His black mid-thigh suit coat, vest, and pants were nicely tailored.

Lost souls? I wondered if they were the couple involved in the sad and horrid wedding tragedy so many years ago.

Their story had been passed down for more than a century. He had served in the Civil War and escorted Lincoln's body to its final resting place in Illinois before walking all of the way home to marry his sweetheart. After the wedding ceremony, their horse drawn buggy overturned and they were both killed.

"Are they like H?" I continued toward the intersection. "Lost souls?"

"*Yes.*"

We reached the end of the street and crossed to the other side. I paused to take in the panoramic view of the quaint, small town that had become an important part of my life. It had given me a sense of belonging to a community where it was common to recognize a familiar face. Its architectural buildings were impressive, the streets neatly kept, and events held by the city helped to make it a cohesive community.

"I sure do like living here, or maybe I should say 'did.'"

My guide simply nodded in affirmation.

It was too early to visit my children and husband. They usually retired later in the evening. Out of habit, I turned the corner and walked to the place where I had spent most of my waking hours.

My Place of Business

I entered the historic brick building and ascended the creaky oak stairs to my office on the second floor.

"It's strange for the steps to be silent."

I looked over my shoulder toward my guide expecting a reply.

"*Yes.*"

Running my fingertips over the terra brick wall above the handrail, I remembered the day when my partner and I wore respirators and were covered in white dust as we took hammers to the old plaster and exposed the beautiful brick beneath. Pausing at the top of the stairs in the reception area, the secretary's desk sat empty.

I turned to the right and passed through the closed oak door of my office. Standing transfixed within the familiar four walls, it had been a while since I had worked in the room. My desk was unusually tidy and neat. Gone were the several stacks of papers tagged with reminder sticky notes making it difficult to see the top of the desk.

A chuckle bubbled from within me as I recalled my husband's reaction upon visiting my office. "How can you work like that?" My method of operation was very sophisticated and could be described it as organized chaos. I knew where everything was and could access a given document quickly. Yes, I am or was computer literate. I had to be with operating a business in this day and age. However, I admit, I had a habit of piling documents in a stack, usually to my right, and would address them at a later time. Call it procrastination. It was my way of pushing the problem or concern to the back of my mind to lull over a viable solution while I focused on something else that needed to be done.

The calendar desk blotter displayed the month that I last sat in my chair, still stained with coffee rings and decorated with ink doodles. A family picture on the front corner of my desk seemed to stare eerily at my empty chair. It was one of my favorite photographs. I placed it where I could see it often throughout my workday. My antique double green globed oil lamp, which sat to the front and in the center on my desk, was free of dust. With my chair pushed into its proper place, it was easy to assume that my business partner had taken the time to straighten and clean my office.

My attention was drawn to the moments of my life captured in the framed photographs on the credenza behind my desk. Seeing the picture of my best friend and me, I remembered the day it was taken. *We were so young.* Our silly and innocent poses brought a smile to my face. I believe we were in high school when it was taken. We continued our friendship after graduation and survived as roommates in college, both majoring in business with minors in English. We took the same classes each semester and purchased and shared one set of books to save money. She was my maid of honor at my wedding and I in hers. With our common fondness for reading and our love for books, we eventually went into business together and began a small press publishing and distributing company. As entrepreneurs, our daily schedules could be easily adjusted to accommodate our children's activities, alternate the responsibility of carpooling them to and from school, and stay home with them when they were ill.

As my illness progressed, I was forced to work from home one day a week, which gradually increased to two and then more. Eventually, the decision to no longer go into the office was made. Even though my eminent death was drawing near, my friend and business partner never complained as her burden increased. During my convalescence, she visited weekly, usually on a Monday, with updates on the progress of our business. By keeping me involved in important business decisions, I suspected it was her subtle way of encouraging me to overcome my illness.

I suspended myself in the seat of my chair and placed the palms of my hands upon the blotter. I thought of the hours I had spent behind this desk. It pleased me to know that the fruits of my labors would be reaped by my family. In the end, I wanted them to have something more than memories. My business offered them financial security, at least for the time being. Sales were going well. I hoped my partner would follow the business plan we had discussed. As a precaution, we tried to plan for the unexpected, a Plan B so to speak. She would deviate from the agenda and set goals as it became necessary.

Going to the window, I looked at the street below. The bird's eye view always revealed an interesting perspective of those who shopped in town. On slow days, I would stand and watch people dart in and out of the stores. Some would encounter a friend and chat for a moment or take the time to talk over a cup of coffee in a cafe. Presently, the sidewalks were void of people.

I crossed the reception area and passed through my partner's office door. Similar to mine in size, her office was neat and tidy as always. On many occasions when I entered her office, she would be singing to music. It helped her to stay focused. Other than the echoing swishing of the washing machine from the apartment next door, the room was silent.

A photograph of her family was on the corner of her desk. Assuming she was home for the evening, I wondered if she looked upon her husband and children and was thankful to be eating an evening meal or watching a movie with them. Maybe my death brought to light the value of time spent with her loved ones. Did she imagine what their lives would be like without her?

I hoped the severity of her grief would subside quickly and be replaced by the good times we shared.

I left her office, went down the back stairway, and entered the warehouse. I passed by rows of pallets stacked with printed books ready for shipment. All was quiet. Was it Saturday? Sunday? We were closed for business on weekends. I turned to my guide.

"What day is it?"

"*In this physical time, it is Thursday, early evening.*"

Ah, everyone is home for the evening. Since my family usually went to bed at a later hour, I thought it would be best to visit my business partner first. She usually went to bed at an early hour and rose with the sun.

"I think I will go visit my best friend."

My guided nodded in approval.

My Business Partner and Best Friend

I stood in the center of her darkened living room, surrounded by antique furniture and oil paintings on the walls. She lived in an older house with its stained wooden trim, a reflection of the Victorian period with its wide base boards, paneled doors, and rosette bullseyes at the top corners of the windows and doorways. It seemed silly to have such a beautiful room but use it seldom. Some of the houses built today do not contain a formal dining room. I admit we only use ours twice a year at most.

I had been a guest in her house many times before, but finally took the time to admire the paintings closely as I toured the room.

A resounding horn, a crowd cheering, and her son's enthusiastic holler of approval for the goal scored in the hockey game he was watching on TV echoed from the family room. I heard the high-pitched giggle of her five year old daughter in an adjacent room and followed the laughter into the formal dining room. The chairs were turned with their backs against the perimeter of the long rectangle table and several blankets covered it entirely. *Oh, a blanket fort. That's the most practical use I have ever seen for a dining room.* It had been years since I had made one with my children.

I was blessed to conceive my children a year after my marriage, while my friend decided to wait a few years before beginning her family. Our pregnancies synchronized when we were expecting our boys. It was nice to share the experience together. I don't know if her daughter was planned or not but remember her excitement when she discovered she was expecting nearly a decade after the birth of her son.

We were like sisters, leaned on each other during difficult times, and celebrated achievements and good times. Our families vacationed together. We were close, very close and I am thankful she was a part of my life.

I could see the glow of a flashlight dancing from beneath the blankets.

"Mama, why are you sad?" The little girl's angelic voice was sincere.

Passing through a blanket, I sat on the area rug next to a big bowl of buttered popcorn, a stack of picture books, and a disheveled blanket. I saw my partner wipe a tear from her cheek.

"I have a dear friend who went to Heaven today." She attempted to smile, hoping to make light of her loss. "I miss her already."

Their orange tabby pushed his nose under the edge of the blanket and sniffed. He slithered inside the tent, went to the popcorn bowl, and sniffed the buttery aroma.

"No, Henry." Her daughter scolded as she rose upon her hands and knees and pushed the cat away from the bowl forcing him out of the tent. She resumed her seat and watched as her mother brushed away another tear. "It will be fine, Mama." Her daughter patted her tiny hand against her mother's arm before pointing to the Candyland board. "It's your turn."

My friend smiled, picked up the dice, and rolled. I assumed the distraction from the thoughts running through her mind was welcomed. She completed her turn and watched her daughter's little hand as it rolled the dice and moved her red game piece to its correct position on the board. It was one of those cherished moments shared by the two of them, together, under the makeshift tent.

The door into the garage opened.

"I'm home." Her husband announced as he juggled his briefcase in one hand and a salad atop of a boxed pizza for dinner in the other. I stuck my head through the blanket to see him enter the mudroom off of the kitchen and close the door with a nudge of his knee. It reminded me of our family dinners. We shared a meal nearly every night when the children were younger. As they became more involved in after school sports, it was a rarity for us to be home for an evening meal. We would often pack brown paper lunch bags, grab something to eat from the snack bar at the arena, or picked-up a quick pizza on the way home from a game.

As the family gathered around the kitchen table, I wandered around the house looking at the family pictures and antiques. I stepped into a small room off of the living room. It was my friend's favorite room in the entire house, her library. She had custom shelves installed on one wall to hold her collection of books. Every shelf was filled with books with the overflow lying atop perpendicular. Had she read every one? Probably, and perhaps some of her favorite books more than once or twice. Scanning the titles, I realized the books were shelved by genre, author, and title. *So, organized.* I expected nothing less.

"Well, hello, dear lady." Greeted a deep, masculine voice.

I turned toward the bay window to see a man sitting behind my friend's antique desk. It was her prized possession. Constructed in the late 1800s, its rich, dark wood reflected the age and beauty of its pedestal design. The pedestal sides were decorated with panels. The top was inlaid with leather decorated with a leaf pattern of gold around its edge, which was protected by a sheet of glass she had custom made. I remember when she purchased it online. She was quite excited when it arrived from

New York. Her husband thought it was for him. Needless to say, she set him straight right away.

The gentleman who had spoken was dressed in a fine suit, Fedora hat, and a cigar clenched between his teeth. He leaned back in the leather desk chair and took a draw from his stogie, making the end glow orange, before blowing a billow of smoke into the air. *Ah, so that's the cause of the cigar smoke my friend often complained about. He looks like a gangster.*

I looked at my guide. He nodded his head once as if to indicate the person was safe to approach. I returned my gaze to the man, who reeked of rudeness and egotism; two of my least favorite qualities in an individual. Did he choose to remain within my friend's house or did his poor lack of character force him to stay within this realm? Either way, I was reluctant to talk to him, so I redirected my attention to the titles of the books on the shelves before returning his greeting.

"You can see me."

"Yes, just as you can see me, sweetheart."

Offended by his endearment, I snapped my head in his direction. He casually took another draw from his cigar and exhaled the smoke forcefully into the air.

"I'm not your sweetheart." I corrected conveying my disdain.

He removed the cigar from his mouth as the corner lifted in a sneer to display ivory straight teeth. He scrutinized my clothing from top to bottom. I surmised he was undressing me in his mind. *Such a cad.*

"I assume you recently died, but as you can see, I did so many years ago." He held his arms wide before straightening the lapels on his dated suit coat.

"You have been given more than three days?" Trying to be kind, I thought I would give him the benefit of the doubt, but assumed he was stuck between lives like the man in the bookstore, for whatever reason.

"In a way, but I would just as soon cross over, as they say, rather than being trapped here any longer." He looked around the room as if his surroundings were below his expectations.

"Why don't you cross over?" Not that I cared.

"I don't know where to go." He rose from the chair and stood next to the desk. He tapped the top of the desk with his stiff left pointer finger. "This was my desk, when I was alive, that is. I was a banker. For some reason I am attached to it. I go where it goes."

"I don't understand. You are somehow attached to it?"

"More like shackled to it." He took another draw from his cigar, exhaled, and motioned with it pinched between the first two fingers in his right hand to the surrounding wall. "Oh, I can move about the house, but as long as my desk remains here, so do I."

I thought back to the man in the bookstore who was comfortable being where he was. It was apparent this gentleman was not. A banker? His clothing suggested he lived during the 1930s or early 1940s, but I knew the desk was dated nearly fifty years earlier. Why was he attached to the desk? Was he a thief being punished for robbing the establishment where he worked? Was he shot during a robbery?

"I don't mean to be rude, but you know you are dead, right?" I stated.

"Yes, sweetheart, I do."

I cringed once again.

"I am curious. If you don't mind me asking, do you know how you died?" I pressed.

He placed his cigar in his mouth, walked around to the front of the desk, and leaned his backside against it. He crossed one polished wingtip shoe over the other, resting it on its toe. Taking a moment to think, he puffed on his cigar and glanced at the books behind me in contemplation.

"Well." He looked at the ceiling as he put his thumb and forefinger on his forehead as if trying to pull the memory from his mind. "I'm not certain of the cause. I was sitting at my desk in the bank. I remember blood coming out of my mouth and nose. I grabbed my handkerchief from my pocket and put it to my face, but there was too much blood. I collapsed onto the top of my desk. The last thing I saw was a large puddle of blood before my vision went black."

"So, you were alone at the bank?"

His gaze returned to my face.

"Yes, after hours. I had stayed late. I was supposed to meet someone, but I died before he arrived."

"I see." *So, he died alone.*

He stood with a slight smile upon his face, as if possessing a secret.

A member of the mob? He certainly looked the part.

"In truth, it doesn't matter how I died. It matters how I lived."

He had a point.

"I agree." I looked around the room. He did not have a guide. Now that I think of it, neither did the man in the bookstore. I turned to my guide.

"Where is his guide?"

"*It has returned home. It was needed elsewhere.*"

"But why has he remained here?" I looked back to the man at the desk.

"*I am not privileged to know the reason.*"

My stark observation revealed the necessity for a guide to escort a person's soul to the other side. I glanced at my protective companion and realized how much I appreciated his guidance to the other side before returning my gaze to the man at the desk. Why had his guide been called away? Were his transgressions so horrid that he was denied further guidance and permission to cross over? I believe God is kind and merciful.

After all, we all make mistakes as we make our way through life. As long as we believe in him, he will welcome us with open arms into his kingdom. At least that is what I was taught in Sunday school.

"So sweetheart, how did you die?" He inhaled from his cigar.

"I was terminally ill."

"You know the people who live here?" He motioned to a family picture hanging on the wall.

"Yes, quite well. The woman is my business partner, or shall I say was."

He scrutinized my face for a moment and shook his hand with the clenched cigar between his fingers toward me.

"Now that I think of it, you have been here before. I remember you."

"Yes, I visited quite often. After all, she is my best friend." I went to the desk and ran my hand over the routed finish on the top edge. "I have always admired this desk. She spent a long time searching for it and was very excited when she purchased it. She could hardly wait for it to be delivered." I traced my finger on the rim of the lampshade of an antique lamp on the front corner, another one of her collected pieces.

"I remember the trek across the country." He took a slow, thoughtful draw from his cigar and exhaled. "I believe she is the third owner. The desk was owned by the bank where I worked. It must have been in their office for a very long time. If you look very closely, you can see a few cigar burns in the leather top." He looked at his cigar in his hand. "I must have knocked it off of the ashtray a few times before leaving my desk."

I bent low enough to examine the charred, amber lines in the green leather. They were small and few in number.

"The bank sold it to a woman. I guess they didn't want to keep the grim reminder of my death in the building. With the employees aware of its history, I doubt many would want to sit at it either. When the woman died, her children sold it to an antique dealer, who in turn, sold it to your friend."

"Do you resent the attachment?"

"At times I do. I miss my friends and I'm a little resentful that they have been able to cross over, yet I have not." He admitted before puffing several times in contemplation. As if struck by his next thought, he grasped the cigar and exhaled the smoke forcefully like steam whistling from a boiling teakettle. "I will not deny, I am curious to see what it is like on the other side." He raised his outstretched arms and motioned to the walls of the room. "Unfortunately, I don't have much choice other than to stay where I am." Lowering his arms, he smirked. "All is not lost though. I have been able to witness several generations come and go and observe the changes in society. The people in this house are nice. They are raising their children to be respectful and responsible. The husband is a devoted father and loves his wife dearly. She is well organized and puts everyone's needs before her own. Personally, I find her quite interesting. Since my day, women's roles have changed a lot. They cooked, cleaned, stayed home, and had children. I never thought much about the time involved in what they did around the house, but thought it was mostly filled with bridge club parties that served finger sandwiches, pie, and tea. This woman runs a household, cooks, cleans, raises her children, and works outside of the house too. I watch her sometime, especially when she is in the kitchen cooking a meal. I look forward to when she makes roast beef. Mmmm …it was always my favorite meal. I usually ate it with a large serving of mashed potatoes and gravy too."

An uncomfortable silence filled the room as we paused in conversation. I looked at the doorway realizing the household was also quiet.

What time is it? Scanning the room, it was void of a clock. Had I wasted precious moments? Knowing this would be the last time I could convey my thoughts to my business partner, what did I want to tell my dearest friend? In truth, there wasn't much that needed to be said. I wanted to encourage her to follow her instincts when making business decisions. She should understand that it eased my mind knowing I was leaving my most capable and trusted friend in charge of our company.

"It was nice meeting you, but I must go." I explained as I left the room abruptly.

I entered her bedroom. My attention was first drawn to her snoring husband, who lay in their antique four poster bed.

The mahogany wood columns were carved with an intricate design. The headboard was at least six feet tall.

The deafening sound caused me to chuckle. It was comical to know I wasn't the only one who slept with someone who snored. Like me, she must have grown numb to the noise, for she slept peacefully.

I looked at my guide.

"You said I can communicate through dreams. How?"

"*As I am communicating with you, imagine it and it shall be.*"

Imagine it and it shall be. I glanced back to my friend. *Imagine it and it shall be.* I stepped to her side of the bed, looked at her peaceful face, closed my eyes, and concentrated.

"What are you doing?"

Opening my eyes, I glanced toward the doorway. Apparently, curiosity had gotten the better of the former banker. He had stuck his head through the doorway and awaited my reply.

Turning to my guide, he nodded his head indicating his permission. I glanced back to doorway.

"I am invoking a dream." I explained before refocusing on the task at hand, only to be interrupted again.

"Why? How?" He stepped into the room, placed the butt end of the cigar in his mouth, and pinched it between his teeth.

"It is a way to communicate with my friend. I want to tell her something before I cross over."

He removed the cigar and opened his mouth to speak again, but I held up my hand in a silent plea to remain quiet.

"I am sorry, but I need to visit my family after I am finished here. Just watch." I restrained the harshness from my voice even though I was aggravated by his intrusion.

He put the cigar in his mouth, crossed his arms defensively over his chest, and stood silently.

I looked at my friend's face nestled upon her pillow and concentrated.

~

I was a small child. The sun warmed my face as I stood on the sidewalk before the line of yellow school buses. My elementary teacher held my hand as we waited. The right side of my head had long blonde hair, while the other half was burnt and my skin charred. I looked at the red pick-up truck to see my business partner sitting in the passenger seat. She turned and looked at me through the rear cab window.

As the teacher and I walked toward her, the burnt half of my head transformed. The skin healed and long brunette hair appeared to match in length to the blonde. I paused before the truck passenger door. The teacher lifted me up to the open cab window. I shrank in size until I became very small, almost fairylike, and teetered on the edge of the door facing my friend. She stared at me before lifting her cupped hands to reveal lollypops. All of them were green in color. Some of them were tiny like Dum Dums, while others were lime Tootsie Pops. One of the Tootsie Pops was unwrapped.

She won't take that one, my partner thought, referring to the unwrapped lollypop.

I had heard her thought while I examined the candy. I smiled mischievously and reached for the unwrapped lollypop. I could tell she was astonished by my choice.

As I drew my knees inward toward my chest and rotated on my bottom toward the sidewalk, a growing concern resonated with her. I paused and looked back over my shoulder at her.

"Do a good job. I am depending on you." I stretched my legs toward the ground and began to slide down the outside of the door.

My partner panicked.

"No, it's too far. You are going to get hurt."

When I landed softly upon the ground, I became the little girl again, and clasped the extended hand of my teacher before turning back at my partner, my friend. I smiled.

~

My friend's eyes popped open as she bolted upright from her pillow. She breathed deeply as if trying to catch her breath. As if reacting to the movement of the mattress, her husband rolled away from her onto his side. She looked toward him, exhaled, and brushed her blonde hair away from her face while she replayed the dream in her mind.

"*One must wake to remember a dream.*" My guide explained. "*Rest assured, she will remember.*"

His words were comforting. I only hoped my message was understood.

"What did you tell her?" The man inquired as he uncrossed his arms.

I thought his bold question was rude. It was none of his business what I told my friend, but I thought I would indulge his curiosity. I stepped toward him.

"We own a business together. Now that I am no longer there to share in the responsibilities, I told her to take care of it." I watched my partner flip back the covers and get out of bed. She took her bathrobe from a hook behind the bedroom door, stuffed her arms into the sleeves, and left the room. The three of us followed as she went downstairs, sat at her desk, and turned on the lamp. She took a small notepad and pen from the narrow, center drawer.

I peeked over her shoulder as she wrote 'Do a good job, I am depending on you' and added today's date at the bottom of the paper. She propped the note against the lamp and shut it off before ascending the stairs to return to bed.

It was reassuring to know she had thought my message important enough to write it down. Maybe she was afraid she would forget it or wanted to keep the message displayed as a daily reminder. Either way, I was thankful she had done so.

The man appeared in the vacant desk chair and removed the cigar from his mouth. He read the note.

"I assume this is what you told her." He leaned back in the chair and looked over his shoulder for my confirmation.

"Yes, my exact words." I glanced over the room one last time. "My job is done here." Making my way to the door, I turned toward the gentleman. "I hope you find your way to the other side someday. I would hate to think you may spend eternity attached to your desk."

"Perhaps someone will pray for my soul and help me cross over. It is doubtful, for alas, those who had known me are all dead. I fear I shall remain here forever, but I could be in a worse place. It isn't so bad." He placed the cigar between his teeth, bit down, and entwined his fingers behind his head.

Recalling what H had mentioned, I made an assumption.

"Is there a portal in the house you can travel through?"

"A portal? I don't know what you mean, but if there was one, it would be of little use to me. I'm still attached to my desk."

True. I wondered if something could be done to help him. I turned to my guide.

"Is he allowed to come with us?"

"*No. I am to take only you.*"

I thought back to my Christian education. Purgatory, a place for lost souls. We were instructed to pray for them.

"Are we in purgatory?"

My guide remained silent. Maybe he wasn't allowed to confirm my assumption whether it be right or wrong.

"Will he ever cross over?"

"*All is not revealed to me.*"

I had no other choice but to leave him behind. I thanked God I wasn't lost, at least not yet. Maybe if I refused to go with my guide on the third day I would become lost. My questions about those I had encountered and what lies beyond this limbo state were increasing within my mind. Were any of my assumptions, correct? Maybe we were just in another dimension that was invisible to those in the physical world where my body remained. The concept was strange, but plausible.

"I want to go home now."

My Husband

I was in the family room. The TV was on a sports channel with a baseball game in progress. As usual, my husband had turned down the volume to a mere whisper. I looked at the snoring man lying on the couch with our cat cuddled up next to him. It was his habit to fall asleep either there or on the floor and come to bed sometime after midnight.

The past few weeks must have been a tremendous strain on him. Maybe he passed out from exhaustion. I was thankful he was able to sleep.

"I was fortunate to have shared my life with this wonderful man. Wasn't I?" I posed the question to my guide.

"*It was as decided.*"

His vague comment piqued my interest.

"What was decided?"

"*As to what choices you made before being born, I do not know.*" He began to explain.

"Before I was born?"

"Yes, it was decided between those you know in this life and in past lives while you were in the spiritual world. Roles each of you would play were decided. You chose your parents, husband, etc., and they chose you as a parent, friend, or wife. However, nothing is set in stone. Decisions you made during your life may have altered your initial path. You had the ability to change its course, whether you did so or not, I do not know."

"Let me get this straight. One of my decisions was to die young?"

"To what purpose, I do not know. Perhaps your death was necessary in order to help someone learn what must be learned."

"And what if they don't learn what must be learned?"

"They must live another life to learn it."

"How many lives have I lived?"

"The number is not important. You will live as many lives as necessary to complete all that must be learned. The total number depends upon you."

"If I have lived many lives, why don't I remember them?"

"The elements you learn in previous lives were not needed for this life. They have been blocked but remain within your mind. As I stated, all will be revealed once we are home."

Past lives? It was an intriguing concept that resonated from my Catholic elementary school years. My teachers, mostly nuns, spoke often of our bodies remaining on earth when we died and our souls going to heaven. The notion was a lot to comprehend as a second grader, but what my teacher had said turned out to be true.

I thought back to an analogy I created when I was seven years old. I was playing in the yard on a warm summer day. I paused while riding my bike to watch my mother arrive home from work and go into the house. I thought each person's life must be similar. We leave home to do our job and when our job is done, we return. My goodness, my insight was correct.

Something brushed against my leg. It was Thomas, our orange tabby who had passed away several years ago. I knelt down and stroked his silky fur.

"Hello, pretty boy. I have missed you dearly."

He circled toward me and brushed his face against my hand. Looking up to my guide, I was curious.

"Has he been here since his death?"

"*Yes.*"

Thomas had lived past the age of nineteen and had grown quite thin just before his death, but as I continued to stroke his silky fur, he seemed younger and healthier now.

I recall the day he entered our lives. Our son was playing in the front yard and he heard meowing. As he looked toward the road, a tiny kitten came crawling toward him. An unkind soul had dumped him off. My son picked the tiny kitten up by his tail and panicked.

"Mom!"

It may have seemed a little mean to carry the kitten so, but I may have done the same. The poor thing was coated with dirt, infested with fleas, weepy eyed, and had mites in its ears. His belly was bloated with worms as well. However, the little attention my son had given the stray had pleased him. Even being held upside down by his tail, the kitten purred. The poor feline had endured a rough start in life, but we ensured the remainder of it was filled with love and kindness.

I have always had a fondness for cats and believe they are little angels sent to those who need them. Why Thomas had arrived at our door, I was certain the reason would be revealed in time. After a quick flea bath, we discovered his fur to be a beautiful shade of orange with darker stripes. His tail had several bands of white toward its tip. A trip to the vet addressed his additional ailments. He was all cuteness and donned a green collar with a bell when my husband arrived home. It didn't take much for the children to persuade their father to allow the kitten to stay and become an official member of our family. They found a box for the kitten to sleep in at night and put a plush towel in the bottom, but Thomas only meowed. He did not want to be alone. After being dumped off by the roadside, I could hardly blame him. My son slept on the floor in the living room next to the box that night. In the morning, I discovered Thomas snuggled in the crook of my son's arm, both sleeping soundly. It was the beginning of Thomas's attachment to my son, his shadow so to speak. He curled himself upon my son's warm lap when he watched TV. He sat at the base of his kitchen chair and begged for whatever was being served for dinner. Every night when I checked on the children before going to bed, the cat was curled upon my son's pillow next to his head.

Thomas was affectionate to everyone in the family, vocally responded when spoken to, and had a way of letting us know exactly what he wanted whether it was through a certain toned meow, a tap of his paw on one of our legs or sitting at the back door until we let him outside for an occasional outing. He was a great mouser and would line up his kill on the doormat. When we opened the door to let him inside the house, he sat as proud as could be looking upward for an appreciative pat on the head for a job well done.

The impact this little furry creature had on our lives could only be measured by the void within our hearts when he passed away. To help come to terms with our grief, we rescued a fuzzy white kitten, Spooky, from a no-kill shelter. However, Thomas's absence was missed most during the preparation of the Thanksgiving turkey. He liked to eat the raw liver. When offering it to Spooky, he would sniff it twice, turn up his nose, and walk away.

I was curious as to why Thomas had not crossed over. I ran the palm of my hand over his back before his ears perked and he pranced away. I rose and turned to my guide.

"Why is he still here?"

"*I do not know.*"

My husband's rhythmic snoring fell silent. I stood, almost holding my breath, and listened as I had done so many times before. When I had trouble sleeping, his lengthy pause in breathing would frighten me. A subtle elbow to his ribs or a nudge to his shoulder encouraging him to roll over and breathe again was my usual remedy. Once he had resumed his normal breathing that was usually accompanied by his incessant snoring, the noise would eventually lull me to sleep.

I was no longer there to ensure he would breathe. Moments ticked by before a snort and gurgle preceded an inhalation of air. I inhaled in unison with him and smiled with relief.

My husband's face had aged some over the years. His charcoal hair was highlighted with gray at his temples and crow's feet enhanced the corners of his eyes, but he was still the handsome man I fell in love with years ago. I admit I was a little apprehensive when he approached me at the fraternity party in college. Since he knew where I sat in class, it made me a little defensive. As we talked during the party, he was able to remove my veil of prejudice to help me see the trueness of his heart. After which, we were inseparable. We studied side by side, earned our degrees, and marred at a young age. We had our ups and down over the years, a few 'discussions' along the way but we had always remained close, best friends, companions for life. Well, for the length of my life anyway. Now that I look back, I'm glad we married young. He was perfect for me in every way, my compliment and confidant. Overall, he made me a better person.

Before we were wed, I received two pieces of advice from my aunt at my bridal shower, good advice. The first, "Don't do anything for your husband the first two weeks of marriage that you don't plan on doing the rest of your life." The first time my husband asked me to make him a sandwich, I told him to make it himself. He did and even made one for me too. Other times, I made one for each of us.

The second was her logical description of the phases within a marriage. "The first third of a marriage, a couple loves each other, the next third of a marriage, a couple hates each other, and the last third of a marriage, a couple needs each other." As I reflect upon our marriage, it was simple to see how we became so busy with the children's lives, we forgot about taking time for each other. We never hated each other, so perhaps we avoided the second phase or maybe moved into the last third because of my illness. We were robbed of growing old together, but maybe it was for the best. I always thought it would be sad to reach the last phase of a marriage, for at that point it would be a question of who would die first leaving the other behind. For us, the question was answered prematurely.

An enlightened thought registered within my mind. I turned toward my guide.

"He knew I would die, didn't he? He knew before he was born, before he met me, before we married."

"*Subconsciously, yes, it was preordained.*"

"He was my provider. That was his purpose." I reasoned as I recalled my illness and his ability to hold the family together while giving financial support.

"*Yes, but it was more than merely providing. He also loved you very much.*"

"I know." I looked at his kind face. "As I did him and still do."

In a way, I got lucky, or maybe I should just look at it as being blessed. I was in my late teens when I met my husband. Blinded by love, I did not realize how wonderful he truly was until we had been married for several years.

We worked together as a team in every aspect of our lives. When I became too busy to do the dishes, he would do them. If he was absentminded and forgot to take out the garbage, I did so. I disliked vacuuming, so he did it. He liked his living environment tidy, which made me want to keep a neater, less cluttered home. Oh, and his lawn. My goodness, it was a carpeting of green without one blade of grass out of place and trimmed neatly. We didn't nag each other for slacking off, or ridicule each other's failures; we just did what needed to be done. I was thankful to have had such a wonderful husband. Each day with him was a gift.

The nightmare of that dreadful day when we sat in the doctor's office holding hands had haunted my dreams for months. As the doctor read my test results confirming my cancer, my husband's first reaction was disbelief. His face masked with numbness as if he received a punch in the stomach, slumping over a bit with his head lowered. Before he turned to me, he sat upright in his chair, lifted his chin, forced a slight grin on his face, and looked me straight in the eye.

"We're going to beat this, you and I." He lifted the back of my hand to his mouth and kissed it.

Unfortunately, we didn't.

He remained unwavering, through the bad times and the worse times. It must have been difficult for him to continue to project a positive and hopeful attitude as he watched me deteriorate over time.

I knelt and kissed his cheek, or at least I thought I did.

"I love you." I whispered, sat back on my heels, and began to concentrate.

~

I sat in a white wingback leather chair in a room with camel brown carpeting and ivory painted walls. It reminded me of the living room in our first house. I had always wanted a white wingback leather chair, but never could justify purchasing one in such a light color. I was dressed in jeans and a sweatshirt with our college logo on it. My husband stepped into the room, stopped, and stared at me. I stood, not knowing how he would react to my presence, and kept my face void of emotion. With each step toward him, I began to fade away like a mist dissipating in a breeze.

"No, don't go!" He pleaded.

I reappeared slightly. My lips did not move as I conveyed my message.

"I want to stay, but I can't. Thank you for seeing the qualities in me that I failed to see within myself. I love you so very much." I faded away, leaving him staring at the empty chair.

~

A snore was cut short as my husband awoke. He sat up, ran his hand through his hair, pulling it back away from his eyes, and looked around the room as if trying to make sense of something.

I watched him rise from the couch, shut off the TV, and leave the room with Spooky following curiously behind him. The stairs creaked as he ascended to our bedroom. He would be lying in bed alone, but then he had done so during my final days in the hospltal. Maybe he would hold my pillow closely and inhale its fragrance. Perhaps it would give him comfort as if I were still nearby.

Reminiscing

I studied the family photographs hanging on a nearby wall, traced my fingertip along the edge of a folded throw on the end of the couch, and wished I could straighten the pile of newspapers on the coffee table.

It was comforting to be in the family room once again. In the later stages of my illness, I was confined to my bedroom until I was taken to the hospital to die.

It was strange to wander around my house in the dark and still be able to see everything as if a light was on. I paused at several family portraits displayed on an end table.

When my husband and I decided it was time to start a family, we adjusted from two incomes to one so that I could stay home with the children when they were young.

I remember those days with fondness and cherish each one. There were times I wished my husband had been able to witness one of the children's cute antics or comments that he had missed while at work. I often made a point of sharing it with him when he arrived home, but I'm certain my description fell short of actually witnessing it.

My 'stay at home' days were structured and routine. After breakfast, the children were dressed. The television viewing was kept to a minimum, except for educational programs. I read to them often, especially before naptime and putting them down for the night. Every Wednesday we would go to the library for story time, select books to read for the coming week, and stop for lunch at a local restaurant. In the summer, we would visit the park and play outside. When the children began attending school, I oversaw their homework time. When they arrived home from school, I would ask how their day went and how they did on their spelling test. They knew I was going to ask and wanted to be able to give me a good report. They may have thought there were times I hovered or pushed them a little too much, but I wanted them to know that I took an interest in what they did. When they began attending school full time, my friend and I began our business. Even though my days became busier, I made certain the children were always my top priority. No one can fault me for trying my best to be a good parent.

My support did not stop at their academics. As they became involved in sports, their responsibility for schoolwork was still emphasized. Their busy schedules helped them to learn two important life skills; prioritize and time management.

As many of us parents do, I became a taxi service. I drove my children to nearly every sporting practice and attended their games to cheer them on. There may have been a time or two when I got carried away by a ruling of the official and they cringed with embarrassment, but I think they appreciated my enthusiasm. At least I hope so. It was sad to think that my place on the bleachers would be vacant. How many times would they look to my usual seat after they scored a goal or achieved a personal milestone to see it empty?

As I looked from photograph to photograph, it was heartwarming to compare the children's growth and physical changes and interesting to see the aging of my husband and myself.

I was grateful to have shared my life with my husband, my love and best friend. In a way, I was thankful I died first. It would have been difficult for me to find the strength to carry on without him but would have done so for the sake of the children. As will he and face good days as well as bad, but he would face them, nevertheless.

I have always considered my children to be my greatest blessing in life. I would watch my pregnant belly move and roll with the life inside of me. I was blessed to be the keeper of their soul, their protector. I thought back to each of their births, that moment when my eyes first saw their chubby faces, and the thoughts that ran through my mind. "She is so beautiful." "It's a boy." I remember hearing their first cry and the relief within my heart knowing they had made it through the birth unscathed. It was comforting to hold their bundled bodies within my arms and watch them stare at something they couldn't quite see.

Unwavering, my husband was my supporter through the deliveries, steadfast at my bedside, and honored to cut the umbilical cords. As each baby lay upon my abdomen, I recall my husband's face masked with wonder as he watched their every movement. He was overjoyed to be a father, as I was to be a mother. When the nurse whisked the baby away after it emerged into this world, he paced the floor and peeked over their shoulders as they wiped away the goo, measured and weighed, and check vitals to ensure all was well. His eyes twinkled with pride as each bundled child was placed in his arms. He cradled them protectively in the crook of his arm and looked toward me with a smile upon his face reflecting the wonder of their creation.

"Look what you did." He held the baby at an angle for me to see its face.

"We did." I corrected.

He placed the bundle babe within my arms, kissed me on my forehead, and called our parents to announce our joyous news. I remember the excitement in his voice as he shared the birth of each baby. *Ah, good memories.*

Time does seem to fly, or do we just get busier? My babies were precious, but most parents probably feel the same way about their children. The time from their infancy to their toddler years passed quickly. Etched in my mind is their first day of preschool when I put on a brave face while secretly holding back tears as I released their tiny hand and watched them walk through the classroom door. At the end of their class time, I waited with the other parents outside of the classroom, anticipating my child's tales of their activities. I was met by their smiling face as they presented their daily project, which was proudly displayed upon the refrigerator once we arrived home. My favorite art projects were their Mother's Day cards made of construction paper, doilies, their painted little handprints, and illegible crayon lettering. They were usually accompanied by a marigold plant in a paper cup. Their pride was transparent as they presented their gifts to me, jumped up and down unable to contain their excitement, and awaited my approval. Each handmade gift was special because it was given from their heart. Many of the cards are buried in the bottom drawer of my dresser. I couldn't bear to throw them away. My family would discover them when they got around to going through my belongings. Since I had held onto them for so long, I hoped they would understand how much each handmade gift meant to me. They would also find where the tooth fairy had hidden their baby teeth, the bittersweet symbolism of leaving their babyhood behind and entering childhood.

I cherished and embraced each and every milestone in their development from infancy. I remember their first step, their first word, their astonishment when they finally went potty in the toilet, learning to color within the lines, reciting and recognizing each letter of the alphabet, learning to write their name, and their laughter as they knew I had let go of their bicycles while they peddled and remained upright. With each accomplished milestone, it brought them a step closer to adulthood and a step further away from their dependency upon me. Those precious moments cast to my memory, and I am thankful to have been there to experience them. My only regret is that I would be absent as they continue with their journey through life. My responsibility as their parent and advisor had come to a premature end.

In the hallway where the children's school pictures were displayed, I admired the kindergarten wallet size picture of my daughter. She was such a cutie when she was little. Her baby teeth smile, pudgy cheeks, and bows in her blonde hair were captured perfectly by the photographer.

A melancholy ache settled within my heart as I recalled her first day of kindergarten. She would be away for the entire morning, not just the two hours as in preschool. I held my tears in check as I walked her to the classroom door and kissed her gently on the cheek. Unafraid, she turned toward the room, but paused to look back at me and waved her tiny hand good-bye. While she attended the morning session, I ran errands with my son and had lunch prepared before I stood outside the classroom and watched the door open. I knelt upon one knee, spread with my arms wide, and caught her as she ran into my embrace. Another treasured memory. I missed the little girl captivated in the picture.

Her precious face matured, and hair style changed as I progressed to each class picture set in the perimeter of the mat. In the center was her 5 x 7 senior photograph. The baby blue sweater she had chosen to wear complimented her sapphire eyes. The photographer's lighting brought out the golden highlights in her blonde hair. She had grown into a confident woman who spoke her mind eloquently. I smiled proudly. It was comforting to see all of the photos in place. Her high school education was nearly complete. Her finals were this coming week. I hope she would be able to focus on doing her best during exams. She would walk across the stage and accept her diploma at the graduation ceremony the following week. Even though I would not be there to witness the ceremony in person, I could take solace in knowing we had arranged her open house party together. She would see it come to fruition as planned. Her college orientation, scheduling for classes, and dorm assignment was scheduled in the summer. I hoped she was looking forward to her college experience and the exciting next chapter in her life. My, time had gone by quickly.

Someone once told me little boys were difficult to raise, much more difficult than little girls. I looked at my son's angelic face in the next picture frame. I disagree. I believe birth order has more of an impact on a child than their gender. I remember how he would mimic his sister and had the initiative to potty train himself so he could wear underwear just like her. Being the baby, he was a mama's boy and 'cling on' so to speak. He was so shy, so very shy. I remember the countless times he would wrap his little arms around my neck to give me a hug and kiss my cheek. He is my sensitive one, always kind and generous to others, thoughtful in many ways, yet very smart.

My fond memory of his timid smile and innocence were captured in his kindergarten picture. I imagine his apprehension and reluctance to follow the photographer's instructions. Scanning the remaining pictures, I came to his freshman photo. The roundness of his boyhood face had disappeared, and the chiseled jaw of a handsome young man was emerging. His shyness subsided as his confidence developed. Friends described him as easy going, polite, and thoughtful. Much like his father, I imagined him fulfilling the role of a worthy husband and father someday. He inherited my natural business sense of thinking, so I assumed he would choose a career in that field after graduating from college.

It was sad to see the two small empty rectangles in the perimeter of the mat and the large one representing his senior year in the center. He would select his clothing for his final high school picture without my advice and when taken, it would complete his school years photographs. I would be absent from his graduation and hoped he would have an open house equal to my daughter's celebration.

He would attend driver's training classes in the fall. In a way, I was thankful to miss the experience of another rookie driver in the family, but I prayed my husband would find the patience to endure it. Goodness, the car insurance rate will increase too.

Had I prepared my children for whatever life may throw at them? Impossible. When they were young, I had taught them to be independent; make their lunches, help with the laundry, and clean their rooms. As my health began to fail, they willingly took on more of the household chores. They would vacuum the house, prepare meals, do the dishes, and ensure the pile of laundry was kept to a minimum. They accepted the additional responsibilities willingly and never complained.

I entered the dining room and peered into the china cabinet. Behind the protective glass were glassware and stemware. I recalled the resonant musical tone of the fluted Champaign glasses we held to toast to our happiness on our wedding day. It would be nice if the children used them for their joyous wedding receptions too. The antique teacups were used for a very special day of dress up and tea with the children. They were so cautious and careful each time they picked up the teacup, brought it to their lips, and returned it to the saucer. That was a fun day.

Pausing, I stared at the most treasured item on display. It was something quite inexpensive, but priceless. The little clay animal with its body molded and shaped by my daughter's tiny fingers. If you looked closely, you could see her fingerprints in the clay. She had made it during an elementary art class. I believe she had given it to me as a Christmas gift or maybe it was for Mother's Day? No matter. My children's handmade gifts were precious and represented their generosity and love. They were displayed proudly for all to see.

I took a step backward and sighed. Here were some of the materialistic items I cherished but were no longer mine. I couldn't touch them or take them with me. I assumed they would be passed onto my children someday. Would they hold the item, look upon it, and remember me fondly? I liked to think so.

I toured the living room, spending a few moments at the various oil paintings I had purchased over the years. It was a passion of mine. I wasn't an expert on art, so I bought what I liked. I was rather drawn to paintings depicting moments in history and landscapes. I found them to be most fascinating, yet intriguing, with each painting capturing the past lives and moments of generations gone by.

I paused before my desk where I had spent many hours in the quietness of the living room reviewing business finances or working on projects. There may have been a time or two when I had fallen asleep in the high-backed office chair when pushing myself to meet a publication deadline.

When my mind would stray from the task at hand, my favorite family pictures were where I could easily view them for encouragement.

The rooms were as I remembered. There was a misplaced pair of shoes here and an empty glass there, but the items indicated my family was continuing with their lives. I stood at the bottom of the staircase and sighed before ascending with my guide following.

I dodged the dirty socks and various discarded clothing upon the floor as I made my way across the room to my son's bedside. Over the years, I emphasized the importance of keeping a neat and tidy room, but his selective listening apparently tuned out my lectures. At this point in his life, it wasn't a priority. I hoped he would accept the responsibility before going away to college. If not, I pitied his roommate, but then again, he may share his dorm room with someone who preferred a similar lifestyle. Maybe when he began to pay for an apartment or purchase his own home, he would take pride in his living environment. Then again, he may need a woman's influence to change his ways.

Thomas was curled at my son's feet. He raised his head and stared at me.

"I see you are still attached to him." I stroked the cat's back and scratched under his chin. Thomas began to purr as I kissed the top of his head before redirecting my attention to my son.

With his back toward me, I peeked over his shoulder to see the profile of his sweet face. No longer was he the shy little boy who once clung to me while others tried to engage him in conversation. He looked more and more like his father with every passing day. By my estimate, he would be as tall as my husband, if not taller. I wished I could be there to witness the big events he would experience in his life. Who would he take to prom? Who would be his first girlfriend? Who would he marry? I sighed. At least his father and sister would be there to support him and give advice.

My husband's snoring echoed from the next room. I had one more visit before going to his side. I kissed my son's cheek, patted Thomas on the head, and left the room.

I entered her lavender painted room with its frilly curtains and posters on the wall. *Ah, a tidy bedroom.* I looked at the photos of her with her friends she had wedged into the edge of the mirror on her dresser. Within each picture, the girls were in silly poses and laughing. I don't recall having many friends in high school, but it was reassuring to see she did. Was she particularly close to one of the girls within her circle of friends? I don't know. What I did know is that they would all be by her side to see her through this difficult time in her life.

Teddy bears and other stuffed animals sat upon the top shelf of her bookcase. I touched the soft leg of the little lamb. She was two or three years old, had run a high fever, and was feeling poorly the day I gave it to her. I hoped it would comfort her. Apparently, she thought highly of my kind gesture, otherwise she would have discarded it long ago.

I perused the books on her shelves. It was no surprise that she had neatly grouped them by author with the titles in alphabetical order. More than likely, she had obtained the training while working in the media center at school.

At the sound of rustling blankets, I turned toward her bed. She had rolled onto her side, her eyes were open, and she was staring at me. I smiled secretly hoping she could see me.

"*She knows you are here.*" My guide confirmed.

"How does she know?"

"*She can sense you in the room.*"

"Can she see me?"

"*No.*"

"Mom? Are you here?" She whispered as she lifted her head from her pillow.

I looked at my guide.

"Should I answer her? Will she be able to hear me?"

"*Perhaps. Some people, who are sensitive, are able to hear voices.*"

I looked at her eyes that searched in the darkness.

"Yes, it's me." I waited for a reply.

"*Sometimes they can hear you if you speak loudly and close to their ear, although, much will depend on her abilities.*"

I went to the side of the bed, put my lips close to her ear, and increased the volume of my voice as I repeated my reply. I took a step backward and stared at her face, hoping for an indication that I was heard. She continued to stare blankly across the room.

"Perhaps she will hear you when she is between the point of awake and asleep."

Disappointed, I pressed my lips together tightly before glancing at my guide and nodded in confirmation of his suggestion. I was thankful for his hopeful reassurance, went to the doorway, and turned to watch my daughter place her head upon her pillow and close her eyes.

My children had enriched my life far beyond my wildest expectation. I will never regret putting my career on hold to stay home with them while they were little. There were times I doubted my parenting ability. I wasn't perfect. I made mistakes, as most parents do. In the end, however, I learned more from my children than they did from me. I would watch them play and imitate my behavior. It was as if they were little dry sponges soaking up information and reenacting what they had observed. In truth, they were a reflection of me and my husband.

I remember the day my cheeks burned with embarrassment after my son repeated one of my favorite curse words in front of my mother-in-law. The echo of my grandmother's advice 'think before you speak' had returned to haunt me. Realizing that little ears were always listening, I vowed to choose my words wisely from that day forward. I feared my son would go to school, repeat a bad word, and not understand why he was sitting in the principal's office. What would other people think if he said an inappropriate word in a restaurant or church? I imagined the startled glares I would receive from those who disapproved. I assumed his vocabulary would evolve over time and become appropriate for his age. As parents, we preferred he use proper language but understood when 'fitting in' with his peers took precedent. After all, saying 'oh, golly' may seem a little silly to his teammates on the football squad after he was just lambasted by a husky opponent on the field.

As I look back, I know I did my best to instill good morals and values within my children. I am proud of the individuals they are becoming. Pride isn't such a bad emotion, but if not kept in check, it can be mistaken for arrogance. May they stay true to their hearts and experience success in their future endeavors.

I went to my bedroom, sat in the chair next to the dresser, and watched my husband sleep. Spooky was curled at his feet. As the sun peeked over the horizon and illuminated the room, I went to the window and looked to the east. The scattered clouds of the night sky rippled with pink, orange, and yellow. It was a colorful sight to behold, but also indicated I had two days remaining.

Day 2

A Dream Come True

Two days. I wondered what lay ahead for my soul as I scanned the sky toward Heaven, if that is where it exists. A cloud formation in the shape of a horse reminded me of a dream I had years ago.

I was riding bareback atop of a large dapple gray stallion. My fingers were entwined within his mane. At first, I was afraid I would fall from his great height. He was powerful and majestic with his light gray coat splattered with darkened spots on his rump. Long feathery hair hung from below his knees to the ground. It covered his hooves and was muddied with dirt as he galloped. I released my hands from his mane, spread my arms wide, and turned my face upward to the cloudless blue sky. Happy. I was truly happy, even though it was just a dream. Or was it? Had it been a subconscious yearning?

Within a year of the dream, I found him or with the help of divine intervention, he found me.

I received a call from a friend who runs a shelter for horses. An abused dapple stallion had arrived, but she would have to turn him away because the shelter was overcrowded. On a whim, she called me.

"I think you should take a look at him. He would be a perfect fit for you."

I took a quick glance at my appointments for the day, found nothing pressing, and told her that I was on my way.

My expectation of a beautiful dapple waiting patiently for me in the stall was a far cry from what I encountered. He stood still with his head hanging low, a look of defeat. He appeared depressed and in pain. He had yet to be examined by a vet. After a close inspection, I knew his unshod hooves were an easy fix. His gray coat was matted with mud and his mane and tail tangled with burrs. Even the feather fur around his hooves was solid with burrs and mud, but his legs looked straight and in good condition. A bath and grooming would clean him up for a closer examination.

I stepped into the stall and approached him. He stood still as if he didn't have the energy to move. His eyes rotated in my direction as he waited. I extended my hand, palm facing me, and reached for his forehead. He closed his eyes as if my soft touch was welcoming. I stepped closer and began to stroke his neck.

"Hello, big boy. You have been through a lot, haven't you?" I continued to stroke his filthy coat as I circled his body. I cringed as my hand skimmed over his protruding hip bones and could count the ribs on his side. He would need time to put on weight and recover his strength. I wondered if he would ever be able to trust a human being again. Would he be able to trust me? He was impressive, standing seventeen hands high and true to my dream in every way except for his current state. To me, he was beautiful.

As I completed my once over, I turned to my friend.

"You're right. He's a perfect fit. Please call the vet. I'm going to get him bathed and combed out."

After gathering a bucket of warm water, soap, a sponge, and comb, I washed away the filth. Cleaning him up was easy. It would take more of an effort and patience rebuilding his spirit. Was it a coincidence that he had the same markings and coloring as the stallion in my dream? I was able to have him fully bathed and began untangling and combing his mane when the vet arrived.

After a thorough physical, a remedy was planned for the horse's medical needs. He was put on a strict diet. His hooves were addressed by a farrier. In accordance with the vet's instructions, the horse was too fragile to move. He was temporarily tethered in an alcove of the barn until he was strong enough to be transported for boarding at a nearby stable. I visited him several times a day hoping to earn his trust and strengthen the bond between us. When he was fit, I worked with a trainer to ensure he was saddle ready. I exercised him as often as my schedule allowed but made a habit of presenting him a carrot or two before our Sunday ride. Good times, just me and my horse.

When my illness began to weaken and ravage my body, I hired a groomer to exercise him on a daily basis. At least I could rest assured he was in the best of care.

The children's bathroom door closed, drawing my attention. I turned away from the window to see my husband open his eyes. He threw back the blankets and headed toward our bathroom.

My family had a long day ahead of them. I had planned for the viewing today and the burial tomorrow. I didn't want to drag out my funeral over several days. The quicker I was in the ground, the sooner my family could resume some type of normalcy.

Knowing my family was preoccupied, I needed to see my horse one more time. Closing my eyes, I pictured my next destination.

Inhaling the familiar odor of horse and barn, I opened my eyes to see riders exercising their horses in the arena of the boarding stable. I missed the unified solitude with my stallion.

Most riders began early in the day, a display of their dedication to their animal. Many were practicing for a show while others rode for pleasure. I had ridden for pleasure, for time with my horse was one of the few things I did just for me.

I went to his stall. He was eating hay from the mesh bag hanging on the wall. My spirit guide stood nearby, alert and scanning like a radar in search of danger. He remained silent as if respecting the privacy of my thoughts.

"Hey boy, how are you doing?" I reached upward and skimmed my hand across his rump as I stepped to his left side. He had been brushed recently. The waves in his mane cascaded downward without a single tangle. The hair over each hoof was clean, brushed, and feathery soft. I patted his muscular shoulder. Even though his size was intimidating, he was gentle and obedient to the slightest of commands. I watched his ears flip forward and backward like loose shutters on a window. He was listening to something or someone within the stable. He turned his head toward his stall door as he continued to chew. I wondered if he anticipated my arrival or if he even missed me. Maybe he would be visiting a local charity today. I had signed a contract permitting the boarding stable to use him as a therapy horse for special needs children, the elderly, and veterans. At least he would continue to receive plenty of gentle attention from others and have a purpose to his life. I had left enough finances in his account to ensure he had a place to live for a while. I hoped my daughter would take an interest in him, but with her going away to college soon, her priorities were elsewhere. As his funding ran out, my husband may be forced to sell him. Maybe the stable would keep him on as a therapy horse. Whoever ended up with my mighty stallion was certain to have a gem of a companion.

He turned back to the hay bag and pulled another mouthful through the mesh. I gave him one final pat on his shoulder before I left his stall and nearly stepped into the side of a passing horse being led by a groom.

A whinny drew my attention to a horse I had often admired. It was a majestic ebony Friesian stallion. It was tethered while its rider expertly saddled him as if he had done so many times before. Climbing atop of his mount, he reined him toward the arena. The spirited animal nodded his head and flipped his tail as it pranced in anticipation. Its rider sat tall in the saddle as he eloquently controlled the horse and directed it through its exercise routine. *Such power, such strength*. I often thought of having such a horse but feared I would be unable to control it.

In the next stall was an elegant Gypsy Vanner. It was white and chestnut with a flowing mane, tail, and long hair on its legs from its knees to the ground. The breed involved constant maintenance. Its height was a little too short for my liking. It was beautiful, but compared to my horse, it seemed like a pony.

I turned to watch a gentleman lead a large chestnut mare with a small girl atop. I had to chuckle. The child was so tiny, maybe three years old. She wore a riding helmet, a black jacket, tan pants, and black boots. Her legs spread wide over the saddle with specially made stirrups supporting her teeny feet. She was receiving a riding lesson. Either she had a generous sponsor or a wealthy family member who provided her with the best clothing and expensive riding lessons.

A snow-white kitten tiptoed along the sandy stable floor next to the edge of the stalls. *Another stray.* I had taken in many over the years. One spring, we had five kittens living in our home. They were entertaining, but my drapes were never the same. I helped them find homes and the unwanted ones were brought to the stable. Barn rats and mice are always a problem, so the stable management welcomed the cats and ensured a veterinarian oversaw their health. Many times, a volunteer would discover a dead rat nearly the size of an adult cat. Either one of the cats had killed the varmint or it met its demise under the hoof of one of the horses.

The affectionate antics of a black cat rubbing its face and arching its body against a curious horse's nose brought a smile to my face. The horse nuzzled the cat in return. They seemed to have a special relationship, an interspecies friendship.

"I am going to miss my horse and this stable." I commented to no one in particular before turning to my guide. "Are there horses in heaven?"

"*What do you think?*"

"I recall a story of Jesus coming down from Heaven in a chariot pulled by white horses, so I will choose to be optimistic and say yes, at least I hope so."

With one last look around the stable, I knew I needed to move on. *What do I want to see next*? It would be nice to see where my body will be taking a dirt nap.

"I think I will visit the cemetery."

My Eternal Resting Place

I stood on the empty plot topped with plush green grass where I presumed my eternally resting body would be cold and wrapped in darkness six feet beneath the ground. I scanned the nearby headstones.

"It's depressing. Such a loss of life."

"*What once was is no longer. Only the bodies remain and turn to dust. Those who believe in Him are with Him.*"

It was easy to identify where the graves of the children were located. They were decorated with stuffed animals, trucks, dolls, and balloons that shifted in the breeze. Some were donned with solar lights. Maybe the parents hoped to ease their child's fear of the darkness by having a light ever-present.

Scanning the small graves, sadness overwhelmed my heart. It seemed unfair for them to die at such a young age, to have their lives cut short, and never experience life to its fullest.

As a parent, I was thankful to have been spared the pain of grieving the loss of a child. However, it made me wonder.

"What of infants and children who are too young to believe in Him?"

"Those who are unable to choose Him are with Him, for all that remains here are their empty vessels." My guide gestured to the graves below us. *"They are greeted on the other side by loved ones who have gone before them."*

I tried to read each name on the markers as we continued to walk amongst the graves.

"I have always had difficulty understanding the reason for a stillborn child, one that is aborted, or dies at a young age. It is comforting to know their innocent young souls are safe."

"All that is created by Him has a purpose. Just as you had a purpose."

I stopped walking, but my guide continued until he realized he was alone. He turned around.

"You mentioned that before. My purpose?"

"Yes. Like all others, you existed in order to learn, teach, or create. Perhaps you had to do all of the tasks in order to fulfill your purpose."

"And when our purpose is fulfilled…we go home."

"Yes."

"Do we stay there for all of eternity?"

"Perhaps, once you have learned all there is to learn. Otherwise, you are reborn."

"Reborn? I don't understand."

"Those who have learned all there is to learn remain with Him unless they become a spirit guide or there is another purpose for their return. Perhaps they return to teach something to someone. Some souls in this world are quite old. Others are quite young."

"Wait, we live many lives?" I tried to comprehend his inference.

"Yes, as many as necessary."

"So, I have lived other lives?"

"Perhaps. In truth, I do not know if you have lived only one life or hundreds of lives. That is up to you and your ability to complete each purpose."

"But I don't remember my past lives or what I learned. How was I supposed to know what needed to be done in this life?"

"All will be revealed by Him."

I tried to keep my voice calm and not convey my frustration.

"You say that a lot."

He sensed my agitation and smiled.

"You may have been aware of a past life subconsciously. Was there a period in history you were particularly drawn to or liked? A style of music? Experienced an internal urge or desire to travel to a particular country? All may be a part of your past."

My favorite pastime was shopping for antiques. Was it a coincidence to find myself attracted to certain items? I had a passion for Victorian furniture, paintings, architectural pieces, rustic wooden bowls, and wooden buckets. Could they have been items I used in a past life or merely clues as to when I had lived? The items seemed to fall into two historical time periods: Victorian and in a way, medieval. I often wondered what it would be like to live in a castle. Dirty, perhaps, but the romantic within me looked beyond the unhygienic conditions. French, I had always wanted to speak the language and Latin too.

"England." I whispered, walking back to my plot.

As a teenager, I was drawn to detailed Victorian items and architecture. Could I have lived in London during that time period? I had always wanted to travel there, but never did.

"Did I live in England?" I inquired over my shoulder.

"*It is a possibility.*"

I glanced up at the angelic face of an angel statue poised upon a fluted pedestal. Its solemn expression looked down upon the grave below. I crouched to read the engraved name and date. The woman had died nearly a hundred years ago. She had lived most of her life in the nineteenth century. Maybe she had known the man in the bookstore.

"History has always intrigued me, especially medieval history. Scotland. For some reason I was drawn to the city of Edinburgh. I would have liked to stay in the castle for a night. In truth, I probably wouldn't have slept, but wandered the halls exploring and imagining the stories each room could tell."

My guide closed his eyes and looked upward. He nodded his head and looked toward me.

"*He gives his permission.*"

Pictures flashed within my mind, a vision from Him. My questions were answered. I began to pace the graveyard as I explained what was revealed.

"I was in a small chamber set apart from the bedroom." I began to describe the scene within my mind. "There was a fireplace, and the walls were made of wood panels. The room was in a very old building, a castle." I stopped pacing and looked at my guide for confirmation, but I received none. The flash of pictures continued within my mind. I resumed pacing and let my hand touch the top of each gravestone as I passed. "I was present at a birth, but I wasn't the midwife. A baby was swaddled in linen, placed within a second linen trimmed with eight-inch handmade lace. The infant was handed to me by a woman. As I looked down at him, I caught a glimpse of the rigid black bodice I was wearing. I stared at the baby and realized I was holding James I." I glanced at my guide from the corner of my eye. "I was present when a king was born." *I was in the presence of royalty?* "I handed the infant to one of the three women standing behind me. Light from a window gave them a shadowed appearance. I redirected my attention to the woman who had just given birth. There were six women in the room including a midwife, all wearing black gowns." I stopped and stared at my guide. "I was in Edinburgh Castle and Mary Stewart had just given birth to a baby boy." I tried to recall the research I had done on medieval history. "He was Mary Stewart's son, James VI, King of Scotland, who would succeed Queen Elizabeth I and become James I, King of England and Ireland." I looked at my guide for confirmation. It wasn't necessary. I was quite certain I was correct.

"*Yes.*"

"If I was present at the birth of James VI, then I must have been one of the four women of her court." I reasoned searching my memory. "I had to be the closest to her, the most important." *Oh, what were their names? Mary Beaton, Mary Seaton, Mary Livingston and….* "Mary Fleming, right?"

My guided nodded his head in affirmation.

"I believe Queen Elizabeth I, Mary Stewart, and I had the same grandfather, James IV."

"*That is correct.*"

I rambled on.

"Oh my, I was royalty. My mother was Mary's governess. For the young Queen's protection, we lived in France a decade or more." *No wonder I wanted to learn French and Latin. The desire was almost a confirmation that I had once known the languages proficiently. They were probably blocked within my mind.*

"I don't recall much other than that."

"*What did you learn in that life?*"

Learn? I tried to think, to recall my past life, but pieces were missing. A flash of pictures flooded my mind again as if I was being allowed to see what was needed. I was a few years older and was in Edinburgh Castle, but then tragedy struck. The castle was attacked and overthrown by the English. I saw a man tipping a vial upward and dumping its contents into his mouth. *Poison,* to forgo the agony of being tortured. He was carried out of the castle on a stretcher as I walked beside him. I assumed he was my husband. *What about children?* I pictured two of them, a boy and a girl, but they were absent. For their safety, maybe I had sent them to a close relative or possibly to France. I must have had reliable connections to call upon during the violent crises. But what happened to me? My imagination tried to fill in the void of information. Was I thrown into the streets? Did I go to prison? Perhaps I did not need to know that part of my life.

What did I learn? I remember the ridicule and humiliation from those I passed in the street. Maybe they thought I had received what I deserved. After all, those of royal blood were always envied by the lower classes. A flash of a memory revealed a dark place lit by sputtering torches. The air was thick with smoke and the putrid stench of sweat and burnt flesh. I put a handkerchief over my nose and mouth to conceal my impulse to gag or worse yet, vomit. The heavy hand of a towering, muscular man clasped my upper arm and pulled me along. It was difficult to keep stride with his giant gait. As my foot began to skid on the stone floor, I looked down just in time to hop over an overturned bucket of feces. From the darkness, a hand reached out toward me. *Was I in a dungeon or prison*? I pulled away from the grungy fingers as they grasped my shoulder.

My guide redirected my train of thought.

"*What emotions do you feel*?"

I looked at my guide. His eyes were locked upon mine as he awaited my response. *Emotions*? I thought of the grungy hand reaching through the bars and briefly clutching my shoulder. I made a face of utter disgust.

"*No, the emotions you experienced within yourself, not toward others*." He corrected as he read my thoughts.

Within myself. It was apparent I was royalty. I imagined I would have lived in luxury. My every need would have been anticipated and met swiftly. I probably lived a life of court, dressed is elegance, donned with jewelry, and ate from a banquet of food at every meal. I bathed regularly using scented soaps and slept upon down or straw filled mattresses in elegantly carved wooden beds in estates across Scotland that were warmed by fires in large stone fireplaces. My pastimes may have been spent doing embroidery, horseback riding, archery, playing chess, and falconry. Yes, it would have been a luxurious life compared to the peasants' lifestyle. To them, I may have appeared to be a bit of a showoff, enjoying the best in life, and even flaunted it to an extent.

My past life seemed like a fairytale, until I recalled the dark day when Edinburgh Castle was overthrown. *Sadness? Fear? Despair?* A man, my husband, admitted defeat before drinking from a vial. *Pity?* I could hardly blame him for ingesting the poison. He was afraid as well and knew he would be tortured without mercy before meeting his fate at the treacherous hands of an executioner. He was taken away to a prison or dungeon, but I can't recall where? I guess it doesn't matter.

I remember finding his body lying on the cold stone floor of his cell. I cared little for the slippery stench I knelt in as I picked up his head and cradled it within my lap until his struggle to breathe fell silent. *Was it compassion I felt for him, or love? Grief.*

I was stripped of my wealth, which included jewelry given to me by the Queen. *Humiliation.* Even though my possessions had been confiscated, they couldn't take away the royal blood running through my veins. I would always be of the upper class even though I was no longer living as such. *Pride.* Did I stand trial? Was I allowed to reside in my dead husband's estate, or did a relative take me in? Did I remarry? More than anything, I was curious to know how I died.

A picture flashed in my mind. The sun filtered through the windows adjacent to the head of the bed which was against a wall in a wood paneled room. A fire crackled in the fireplace on the opposite wall from the bed. The room seemed warm and quite comfortable. I stared down as my spirit floated above it. Sitting in a chair next to my bed was a woman holding my hand.

"I know her, don't I?" I looked at my guide.

He nodded to indicate I was correct.

"I knew her in this life, I mean the one I just lived, didn't I?"

"Yes."

She's young. Her kind face with its ivory skin made her seem like a porcelain doll, but the woman I knew in my most recent life possessed a skin tone of chocolate brown.

Once again, my guide read my thoughts.

"*Yes, she is one in the same.*"

"She chose to be a woman of color to teach something to others, hasn't she?"

"*Yes, but you have yet to tell me what you learned from your medieval life?*"

I scanned the emotions I had experienced and tried to convey them as best as I could.

"Overall, it was humbling. Even though I was royalty and lived a lavish lifestyle compared to others, I learned I was no better than they were. Only our circumstances separated us. I was blessed but did not appreciate it. I was eventually forced to depend on the generosity of relatives after my flamboyant pillar in society had crumbled beneath me. My children taught me to put their needs above my own. My heart swelled with compassion when my husband suffered from the effects of the poison and died in my arms. I experienced empathy and helplessness when my Queen was executed before my eyes.

Above all, I remained loyal to my husband and Queen and grieved their passing. I experienced many emotions, and taught others that sometimes those who place themselves high in society may eventually take a fall. I wonder if anyone felt sympathy for my plight. Maybe I had to learn to rise after the fall?"

"Yes, and what of your Victorian life?"

As I thought of my Victorian life, elements of my personality were verified by the pictures that flashed within my mind. I used my prestigious place in society selfishly. I would just as soon step on someone to attain my goal than to pull them along and help them rise with me. I think in today's society, some may classify my personality as aggressive. I was an excellent example of how not to treat others. I was a villain and disliked by many. Perhaps I had learned how offensive my personality was to others because I had little tolerance for anyone who possessed such a quality now.

"I wasn't a very nice person. Was I supposed to teach others something?"

"Perhaps."

"As far as the emotions I experienced, selfishness is all that comes to mind. My stature in society was quite high, but I abused the power of the position for my own benefit."

My guide remained silent.

I scanned the gravestones once again, knowing the remnants of each person lay cold within the ground. Was there a lesson they taught others, did they learn something during their life, or did they accomplish both? It was reassuring to know their souls continued on, they aren't dead, and possibly have moved on to their next life. Each grave marker was just a place to remember a person existed, to have somewhere to recall their life, and to grieve.

What of my life? What had I learned? What did I teach others? Had I done anything worthy of remembering?

"*Your conclusion*?"

"Even though I have had many lives, my physical body, whether fat or thin, and what I did to make a living, royalty or peasant, and how I died, are not important. What is important is teaching and learning in order to fulfill my purpose. Above all, the emotions I experienced are what I take with me when I leave each life."

My guide nodded his head as if pleased with my answer.

I noticed the shadows had elongated upon the ground. Stopping at my plot one last time, I stared at my final resting place and sighed.

"I need to go to the funeral home."

The Funeral Home

As I entered the large room, whispered conversations surrounded me. People stood in small clusters. Two elderly women stood before my casket. Others sat on folding chairs. Since my death was eminent, no one was crying, except for one. I glanced toward the ceiling in disgust. *Seriously, Mother.*

As requested, my body was donned in the dress I had selected. Candelabrum with a single candle resembled bookends at the head and foot of my casket. The flame in their red sconces danced and flickered like guardians protecting my soul. All in all, it was a typical viewing room; neat, tidy, and a little conservative with boxes of facial tissue placed upon various tables.

Easels set around the perimeter of the room displaying poster boards with photographs of captured moments of my life. I approached the nearest easel and examined each picture closely. Most of them were of my husband, children, and me. Each photograph rekindled a memory within my mind. There were pictures of birthday celebrations, opening gifts on Christmas morning, picnics, vacations, and the children in Halloween costumes I had handmade. My sewing skills were poor, but I knew how to sew a straight line and was able to manage the attachment of a zipper or two. My children were thrilled with the finished creations, maybe even surprised. In a way, I surprised myself. *Aw.* I smiled at the photograph of myself in a hospital gown and a swaddled tiny baby held protectively within my arms. I looked horrid, but many said I looked great for having just given birth. It seemed so long ago. My babies, who were once so tiny, are now nearly adults.

There were also pictures of my wedding. Goodness sake, I actually thought my dress was pretty then. My, styles have changed. And I look so young, and thin too.

Family … it means everything, through good times and bad. Some of the pictures captured us in silly poses. Several of them were candid shots of me. My shoulders were scrunched upward toward my ears, a grin on my face, and my right hand was raised as I waved my fingers toward the camera. It was my go to pose when I was being foolish.

Dozens of flower arrangements sat upon the floor or atop small pillars near my casket. Their ethereal fragrance diffused tranquility within the room. I read the card on a lovely bouquet of lavender roses. The sentimental and kind words touched my heart.

I once heard someone say you should only give flowers to a person while they are alive because the dead can't appreciate them. Many believe the expense is a waste of money. They are wrong on both counts. I scanned the various arrangements and bouquets and was grateful for each sender's arrangement, no matter how big or small. Their uniqueness of color and beauty represented the individual's grief and empathy within their heart for my family.

"She looks nice." An old woman whispered behind me.

"I agree." Another elderly woman replied.

My eyebrows rose upward in recognition of their aged voices. I turned to see the most pessimistic and frugal persons in town who never spoke a kind word to anyone. As a reflection of my character, I had made an effort to treat them with respect whenever our paths crossed at church, in a store, or on the sidewalk in town. They were known as the town busybodies and made a point of knowing everyone's business. Over the years, they had approached me several times for donations from my business for church committees in which they served. As a supporter of my community, I gave a just and fair donation to their cause. During coffee and donuts after Mass, I often observed them sitting alone at a table. I assumed they liked to gossip about those who entered the hall.

I hoped my kindness and generosity inspired a need for them to pay their respects, but knowing their reputations, I suspected they were here for another purpose.

I searched for my husband and hoped he was monitoring the women. Unfortunately, his back was turned while he talked with an elderly couple.

Hovering behind the women, I listened. I had to admit, eavesdropping on a conversation when you are invisible has its advantages.

"Her hair could use a coloring." One of the women scrutinized my hair as she leaned over my body.

"That was rude." I turned to my guide. "What a cruel thing to say. It's my natural color."

He remained silent.

"Her bracelet is lovely." The other old biddy lifted it from my wrist to examine it closely. It was yellow gold with two silhouette charms: one representing my daughter, the other my son. Each charm was engraved with their name and date of birth. The bracelet would be removed before my burial with each of my children retaining their charm.

"I swear, if I wasn't as stiff as a board and my fingers intertwined with the rosary, she would slip the bracelet from my wrist and keep it for herself." I hoped she wouldn't find the clasp as she continued to rotate it between her fingers. The women acted like vultures circling their next meal.

"Hello." My husband greeted the women, who were startled, dropped the bracelet back into place, and turned in unison toward him. "Thank you for coming." He extended his hand toward them.

Thank goodness. He comes to my rescue even when I'm dead.

Moving onto the next easel, it was filled with more candid shots. I had completely forgotten about many of them and examined the backgrounds to remember where each had been taken.

A looped video played my favorite songs while displaying photographs of my life. It was a nice tribute and easy to see my daughter's creative touch in its making.

"The last month was very bad." The emphasized drama in her boisterous voice caused many to look in her direction.

Oh, good lord. How would she know? I haven't spoken to her in years.

I expected my mother to attend my viewing and funeral, even though I preferred she didn't. Like everyone else, she needed to say good-bye. However, her mannerisms were inappropriate and embarrassing. She commanded everyone's attention with her clamorous comments, dramatic display of dabbing a tissue to her puffy eyes and runny nose and spoke through her tears about something she had little knowledge of, thus playing on the sympathies of those nearest to her.

"It would be nice if she would whisper like everyone else." I commented to my guide, who continued to remain silent.

Maybe she carried a hidden guilt for leaving things unsettled between us, not that I cared. In fact, I preferred it that way. I watched as she tried to convince everyone of her sincere love for me.

"Well, I wasn't allowed to see her, but from what I understand she was quite a handful. She became mean, very mean toward her family."

Oh, I wish she would shut up.

"She would yell at them, call names, and refused to see me." Mother's bottom lip quivered. She held the tissue to her mouth to disguise a sob.

"Well, she got one thing correct. I didn't want to see her." I confided to my guide before feeling the need to justify my reasoning. "She thinks she is an expert on how I should or should not have lived every aspect of my life. The day finally came when I could no longer tolerate her toxic personality, so I walked away from her. No longer did I visit or answer her phone calls. It's not as if I hate her in any way. I was tired of the drama she created. I had grown weary of her criticizing my decisions, giving me her unwanted advice, and telling me how to raise my children. She had little patience for me when I was a child, so how could she be an expert on rearing little ones? Bottom line, she is a control freak and I no longer wanted to be controlled."

Mother had barely taken a breath before she continued.

"She was defiant, refused help from others, and wouldn't follow the orders of the nurses and doctors. And she would have these crazy dreams and call people on the phone and tell them unbelievable things. Then she would accuse them of being liars, gossipers, and such and then tell them they weren't allowed to visit her in the hospital." She began to cry again.

A little gray hair lady tried to console her.

"I knew someone else that became the same way toward the end of their life. I think the medications the doctors had prescribed were the cause of such behavior. Or maybe it is a way of their brain shutting down, telling their body it is time to die. Either way, it's not their fault. They hardly know what they are doing at that stage of their illness."

My mother's face contorted in shock. She stared at the woman as if she had said the dumbest thing in the world. I was quite certain the logical train of thought never entered her mind. After all, she wasn't the sharpest knife in the drawer, even though she thought she was.

I laughed out loud. It was nice to see her know-it-all attitude put in its place.

Unable to withstand the drama any longer, I stood behind a group of chairs where my children were sitting with their friends and talking quietly. Thankfully, their topic of discussion was something other than my death. It was nice to know they were surrounded by supportive friends.

It's human nature to protect your loved ones. If I could have spared my children from the experience of watching me die, I would have. I glanced at my guide and recalled what he had stated. My children chose me as their parent and possibly knew I was going to die at a young age. Were they to learn something from my death?

I am proud of the way my children handled my illness. Even though I was unresponsive toward the end of my life, they overcame the sadness of my condition and continued to visit me. It pleased me to know that they were present when I took my last breath.

Unbeknownst to her, a woman passed through my spirit and continued on her way across the room. I wondered if she had experienced the coldness of my soul or maybe she assumed the temperature change was a draft from the air conditioning.

The room was near capacity. I recognized most of the people but scanned the sign-in book on the pedestal for unfamiliar names. Mass cards were neatly stacked to one side of the pen holder. Just as I had planned, my favorite saint was printed on it. I assumed the psalm I selected was on the reverse side along with my name, date of birth, and death. I turned to my guide behind me.

"We will have to return here tomorrow before the Mass."

"As you wish."

I eavesdropped on conversations as I moved about the room. Many of their comments were the same.

"She is at rest now."

"Her suffering is over."

"She looks good."

Really? Did they expect me to be dehydrated and shriveled up like a raisin?

"It'll be all over soon and then life will get back to normal again." A stoutly woman commented.

Normal? I wondered if the woman considered her nonsensical comment before she spoke.

"It will be different, my family will adjust and continue on, but I doubt life will ever be normal for them again. It will be a new type of normal, but not as before."

Meandering to the next group, I listened.

"She led a good life."

"She was a wonderful person."

"She helped so many people."

"She was a kind and generous person."

"Our charity could always count on her."

It was nice to overhear their comments, but it would have been nicer for them to say them to my face when I was alive.

As darkness began to blanket the windows, my husband covered his mouth with his hand to hide a yawn. He looked tired. I wished I could hug him and tell him everything would be fine, but I had no guarantee that it would. He glanced at the children, sighed, and ran his hand through his hair before leaving the room.

Assuming he needed a few moments of solitude, I followed him down the hallway and into a side room reserved for the family of the deceased. He approached a table, selected the top paper cup from a stack, and poured himself a glass of water from a pitcher. Other than coffee and toast this morning, the plate he filled with various cheeses, crackers, salads, and fruit was his only other meal of the day. I hoped he would take better care of himself once the funeral was over. After all, he was the only parent the children had left to depend upon. Surely, that thought had registered within his mind as well.

Taking a moment to peruse the various cookies displayed in neat, tidy rows on a tray, he chose a chocolate chip cookie. *His favorite.* I watched him sit at a small table next to a window. Staring at his plate, he exhaled as if releasing tension and anxiety before eating a forkful of macaroni salad. What was going through his mind? Maybe the events of today were too surreal to grasp. Maybe he was tired of the grief-stricken visitors with their bombardment of standard questions or comments and his canned replies. After enduring it for several hours, it would wear on anyone's mind.

"It will all be over soon, dear." I knew he could not hear me.

"Dad."

I turned to see my son in the doorway.

"Grandma is asking for you."

"Of course, she is." My sarcasm was apparent once again. "As usual, she wants everyone's attention as she makes her grand exit. With her aversion for driving after dark, I am surprised she stayed this long."

"I'll be right there." My husband replied as he crammed another bite of macaroni salad into his mouth before washing it down with a gulp of water. His plate of food remained on the table as he left the room.

The clock on the wall indicated the visitation would end within a half hour. *My goodness the day has passed quickly.* I followed him to watch my mother humiliate herself before those in attendance. As usual, she was loud enough to cause everyone in the room to look in her direction and question her sanity.

"You call me if you need anything. Love ya." She threw her arms around my husband and gave him a big hug.

I cringed.

"He probably would like to vomit." I chuckled to myself. "Poor guy."

My mother tried to smile in an attempt to hide her quivering bottom lip. Hugging each of the children before going to my casket, she broke down into tears as she knelt on the kneeler, placed her hand over mine and prayed. Maybe she was asking for my forgiveness, maybe she hoped I was at peace, or maybe she was thankful for the opportunity to be amongst my family again even though the circumstance was a solemn one.

At least my family displayed civility toward her, for what lays in the future remains to be seen. There may be a time when my family may need to depend on her.

She rose. Making her way toward the door, she clasped the hands of those she knew as if taking multiple bows during a curtain call. I could almost feel the entire room let out a sigh of relief as she exited.

Guests bid farewell as visitation hours ended. Within the stillness of the room, my family stood before my casket, bid goodnight to my body, and nodded in appreciation at the funeral director as they left for home.

With little opportunity to return to his plate if food, I hoped my husband would stop on the way home to pick up something to eat.

Darkness crept into the room as each lamp was shut off. Red shadows danced on the walls from the candles that continued to stand guard at each end of my casket. Even though my body was left unattended, it was comforting to know it would not be left in the dark, at least not yet. The dark, how I remember being afraid of it when I was a little girl. It doesn't seem so scary now, only peaceful.

Stepping between the candelabrums, my body's shadowed face looked eerie with the flickering red light upon its features. It looked a little demonic. I wasn't quite certain why the sconces were red. I had always seen several lit upon the altar during mass. Love? I'm certain the color must have some significant meaning.

My requests had been honored; my favorite dress, treasured bracelet, and crystal beaded rosary, a gift I had received on my first communion. I must admit my ensemble worked well.

My husband would keep my rosary and eventually give it to our daughter when the time was right. Knowing my son would prefer a rosary with a more masculine appeal, my husband would pass his rosary to him. We had agreed the rosaries would be a nice high school graduation or wedding gift, but I left the final decision to him.

A thought came to mind as I stared at my body. I did my best to stay in shape during my life. I watched what I ate and exercised often, but the impact of childbirth and aging couldn't be avoided. It is unfortunate that those who are excessively overweight are looked down upon in society. Greed, selfishness, and rudeness are worse characteristics to possess than being chubby. I think one important lesson that I learned during my life is to look at the interior of a person and see them for who they really are. After all, our bodies are nothing more than a vessel that we shed and leave behind.

I returned to the guest book and glanced through the names on the open pages again. I was certain a dear friend would have paid her respects, but her name was absent from the list.

My guide stood nearby and peeked over my shoulder.

"*Someone missing*?"

"Yes, I want to go visit my neighbor."

My Neighbor

Her bedroom was dark. She lay alone in her full-size bed watching TV. As I stood in the corner of her bedroom, I thought of how my husband would be sleeping alone as well and realized that she had been doing so for many years.

It was difficult to pinpoint the emotion I felt - gratitude, friendship, appreciation, and in a way a sisterly bond. Even though she was much older than I, she was my companion while my family maintained their daily activities. She had given me the most precious and greatest gift – her time.

Her stories redirected my focus onto something other than my illness. Maybe her age contributed to her forgetfulness, for she often repeated a previously told story. I didn't mind. I listened anyway.

Her visits were never invasive and as my illness progressed, they were even more welcomed. We would sit together and share stories about our families and friends. She often spoke of happier times when her husband was alive, her childhood on a farm, and her father. Funny, I don't recall her sharing stories about her mother.

She was raised in a household where German was the primarily language, and I assume the only language. On her first day in elementary school, she was sent home and told she could not return until she could speak English. My, times have changed. I am certain accommodations would be made for a child to acclimate them into today's public school system.

She always treated me with kindness, but her deceased husband, family, classmates, and coworkers had witnessed a side of her she kept hidden from me – her temper and stubbornness. Yes, she shared a few stories about a tantrum or two she had experienced. Her habit was to keep her anger bottled up inside, which increased her rage. Her husband would calm her by holding her in his embrace while encouraging her to talk about what troubled her.

Her usual conclusion to her story was 'he was so good for me.'

Her younger years were spent on a farm in Pennsylvania. When she was eighteen, she was ready to leave home and venture out on her own.

"How are you going to make a living?" Her older sister was concerned when she told her she was moving out.

"I want to be a waitress."

"Then do it and be a good one." Her sister advised.

It was all the encouragement she needed. With her family's blessing, she moved to another state, found employment in a restaurant, and rented a two-bedroom apartment. To reduce her rental expense, she sublet the second bedroom to a pair of sisters, a decision she regretted and vowed to never repeat. When she was twenty-one, she purchased her first car, but opted to walk to work instead of spending her money on gasoline.

Her education went no further than the eighth grade. To her credit, the more important lessons were instilled by her parents' lifestyle of frugality and hard work. She watched her pennies and had acquired quite a sum in her bank account prior to getting married.

While working in the restaurant, her male customers would tease her about her single status and try to match her up with one of their buddies. She made a habit of refusing their offers. But one day, a persistent customer suggested an introduction to a friend of his that, he thought, would be good for her. She agreed to meet the man, discovered him to be quite nice, and married him. I'm unsure of how many years they had together, but I remember her telling me that he died of a heart attack within a year of his retirement from work. I couldn't help but notice the sullen tone in her voice when she shared the story of his death. It was easy to see that she missed him terribly. A few years after he passed, a gentleman expressed an interest in her, but she told him straight away she had no intention of becoming someone's cook and housekeeper. Her assumption of his true feelings was correct because he discontinued his unwelcomed visits. I wondered if she ever regretted her decision to remain single.

During our visits, I think she tried to focus mostly on happier times. She often described the house her and her husband built, her attempt to sew a dress with checkered material that ended up looking like a tablecloth, and how the doctor had ordered her to bed rest during her pregnancy with her daughter. While her husband was at work, her helpful neighbor would make meals and pass them to her through her bedroom window.

She often brought me something to eat when she came to visit. I think it made her feel useful, gave her a purpose. I smiled remembering her homemade chicken noodle soup. She made it from scratch and would often describe the steps to make the doughy noodles. At Christmas, she would deliver homemade cookies, many made according to the original German recipes. The large tray contained several varieties and a delicious nut roll. It was the highlight of our Christmas season. Even though we enjoyed her company, we were eager for her to leave so we could each grab our favorite cookie and gobble it up.

As my illness progressed, her stories fell silent. I would watch her lips move, secretly trying to guess which story she was repeating from those I had previously heard. It was kind of a game, but I appreciated her continued effort to communicate all the while knowing I could not hear what was being said. Out of politeness, I would occasionally smile or nod my head as if I understood.

The memory of her hysterically laughing from a silly memory she shared made me realize my illness had at least one purpose - to relieve the monotony of the loneliness in her solitary life.

"She is such a dear person."

"*Yes. She has been blessed with a compassionate disposition and uses it well.*"

My neighbor rolled toward me and stared. Her eyes seemed to be searching.

"I know you are there. I can feel you, but I can't see you." She paused as if waiting for a reply.

My eyes widened in disbelief as I stared at her round and wrinkled face.

"She knows I'm here?" I glanced at my guide to ensure I had not misheard her declaration.

"*She is like your daughter. She has abilities, an open mind. She is a sensitive.*"

"Can she hear me?"

"*Perhaps.*"

"Hello."

She rolled away from me and continued to watch TV.

"Apparently not." Bowing my head, I pressed my lips together and closed my eyes. Being dead was just as frustrating as losing my hearing.

Stalling for time, I went to the other side of her bed. The illumination from the screen enhanced each wrinkle of happiness, or sadness, she had experienced in her lifetime. To me, the etchings represented longevity. My grandmother used to say, "the longer one lives, the more good-byes one says." I could only imagine how many good-byes she had said. I was yet another.

I was thankful for her company, the meals she prepared for my family, and her once a week tidying of my house. Her attentiveness never appeared as nosiness or meddling, only neighborly sincerity.

She clicked the remote. The TV screen went dark. Rolling away from me, she adjusted her pillow and pulled the covers over her shoulder.

I believe it is common for everyone in a marriage to establish a side of the bed in which to sleep. I wondered if she continued to sleep on her side as if her husband was still there. She more than likely did.

Her bedroom was simple and neat, just like her. Her dated furniture, probably the bedroom set she and her husband had originally purchased when they were married, was dust free. I looked at the framed pictures on her dresser and walls. There were several of her granddaughters when they were younger and their high school graduation photographs. Now grown and relocated out of town, they visited seldom. A black and white wedding picture of her daughter with her husband hung on the wall next to an old photo of a man in a suit taken many years ago. I assumed the gentleman was her husband. They seemed to stare back at her. I wondered if she spoke to them when she was lonely and felt forgotten.

I have learned that loneliness is such a sad and cruel emotion.

She would often sit in her favorite chair on the front porch in the twilight of a summer day. It was her way of beckoning for company. I can take comfort in knowing I tried to sit on her sofa glider and listen to her tell her stories as the daylight faded. Maybe she was grateful for the time I had shared with her and felt compelled to reciprocate by spending time with me during my convalescence, but then again, maybe she simply missed me and our conversations.

A photograph of a dog was on her nightstand. She had told me about a dog she had once owned, but its name has slipped my mind. It was a sad story she had shared. She believed someone fed it spun glass and it died. She wished to have another dog for company, but at her age, she denied herself the pleasure in fear of leaving it behind upon her death.

Her rhythmic breathing drew my attention. I went to the other side of the bed and stood near her feet.

"*She sleeps.*" My guide encouraged as he motioned toward my neighbor with his hand.

"There's so much I want to say to her. I don't know where to begin." Exhaling, I plopped down upon the bed next to her shins.

My neighbor opened her eyes, propped herself up on her elbow, and stared at me.

Had I made a depression in the mattress and caused her to awaken when I sat? I would have to wait for her to fall asleep again, but how much time would it take?

Her askance eyes compelled me to speak.

"Thank you for all you have done for me, my dear friend. Thank you for the cookies, your visits, your meals, and your time that means more to me than you will ever know." I sighed knowing she could not hear me, but saying it eased my conscious.

She laid down, adjusted her head upon her pillow, and closed her eyes.

Knowing I had others I wished to see, I stood from the bed and looked at my guide.

"Even though I would prefer not to visit my mother, I feel as if I must."

My guide responded with a nod of his head as if agreeing with my decision.

Mother

The house was void of light and reeked of the old lady perfume she liked to spritz on herself every morning. Her internal clock was programmed to rise with the sun. As expected, she was in bed at this early hour of the night.

It had been quite some time since I set foot inside her house. Not much had changed. The pictures displayed on the wall, the furniture arrangement, and family photos setting upon her desk and bookshelves were the same. As usual, it was immaculately clean.

She married at a young age, a common practice during her generation, and gave birth to me a year later. At the moment in her life when she was blossoming into womanhood, I received the attention she may have wished was directed toward her.

For financial reasons, she worked outside of the household.

One of my earliest childhood memories is one of abandonment. I was quite little, a toddler. I remember walking to the front porch and looking out the glass window of the storm door to see my mother's car backing out of the driveway. I was screaming and hysterically crying for her to come back. I wanted her to stay home and be with me. I turned around to see my sitter, a large woman, scowling with disapproval at my behavior.

It was our family practice to attend Sunday Mass and enjoy coffee and donuts in the church hall afterward. The treat began as a reward for our children's good behavior but evolved into becoming part of our Sunday morning ritual.

After getting my nutty donut and coffee one particular Sunday, I passed by a table of women and overheard my mother bragging about the way she handled one of my toddler tantrums many years ago.

"I was trying to get ready for work. Marie was outside the bathroom door. She was crying and hitting her head on the carpet floor. Well, I just opened the door, slammed her head into the floor, and shut the door again. That stopped her tantrum all right." She boasted before taking a sip of her coffee.

As I sat with my family at an empty table, the pieces of that morning came together. Her lack of patience, constraint on time, and poor parenting technique was a precursor to me crying at the front door as she left for work. Apparently, I was having a bad day, but I was so little and all I wanted was a few moments of her time.

Our relationship could be described as distant and dysfunctional. I don't recall the words 'I love you' being uttered from her lips, a single embrace, or a kind word of encouragement throughout my childhood. I grew up in a world filled with criticism. If someone paid me a compliment, my mother's next breath injected venomous words into my heart that deflated it like the air being released from a balloon.

I think deep down inside she was proud of me and my accomplishments, but for some reason couldn't admit it to my face. Jealously was my only explanation for her behavior.

On occasion, I would overhear her boast to one of her friends about something I had done. There were also unexpected visits to my house where she would take it upon herself to bring a friend and play tour guide as she pointed out my decorating skills. I found this to be quite rude and inconsiderate.

As a child, I looked at my mother for guidance. Doesn't every child? Out of respect, I tried to get along with her throughout my teenager years. It wasn't easy.

It took quite a few years and many embarrassing moments before I learned to never confide any private information in her. Gossiping was her favorite pastime. Once obtaining information, private or otherwise, she would no sooner get off the phone with one person then telephone another relaying what was divulged as if it was a hot potato she couldn't hold in her hands. Sometimes she would embellish her tale with her exaggerated opinion. Eventually, her twisted stories would return to my ears. Didn't she realize her gossiping was hurtful?

Her inability to filter out confidential information was contemptuous. Without my permission, she spread each intricate facet of my life to anyone who would listen. Too young to understand, I mistakenly would share something personal with her. It wasn't long before I finally learned my lesson.

One of my most embarrassing moments was when my mother and I were shopping in a department store. We had met a group of her friends who were also shopping together. My mother immediately began a conversation and before I knew it, she blurted out that I had finally started my first period. I was standing next to her at the time and could feel the heat rise in my face. She went on to explain that I was nearly fourteen and a half years old and it was about time I fell in line with the rest of the girls in my class who had started their periods nearly two years ago. With the added explanation, I was certain my blushed face deepened to scarlet. I secretly wished I could conjure a hole in the floor, drop inside it, and hide. My public humiliation was the beginning of the end of what little relationship we had.

Once the children were born, she became an uninvited meddler whose opinions on how to raise them instilled unnecessary drama and hurtful feelings of incompetence within me. Her overbearing personality tried to control my every decision by telling me what I should do and conveyed her anger when I didn't do as she had instructed.

As she approached the sixth decade of her life, she was compelled to express her affection toward me. Her 'love ya' soured my stomach each time she uttered the words that seemed insincere. Was it an attempt to ensure her soul would be allowed through the gates of Heaven or did she long to hear the same words reciprocated by me and my family?

After enduring a lifetime of her obnoxious antics, the day finally came when I had reached a breaking point. Our last encounter involved several phone calls where she conveyed her displeasure in my inability to follow her orders. Over the next few weeks, she called me several times. Thank goodness for caller ID. I refused to answer, but she left voicemails anyway. Her first message was one of confusion and the assumption of miscommunication, but the last message was direct as she became aware of my refusal to receive and return her calls. I stopped communicating with her all together and simply walked away from our relationship, purging her toxicity from my life.

Do I love my mother? It is a question I have asked myself many times. Maybe, in my own way or maybe I should define it as nothing more than respect.

There were times I couldn't help but to feel sorry for her. I even wondered if others saw her as I did and were secretly laughing at her. My mother may appear nonsensical and silly to many, but her friends held her in the highest of regards. I admit she possesses many redeeming qualities; hard working, kindhearted, generous, and thoughtful, which I admired.

With the understanding that we all face challenges throughout our lives, some force us to learn and some make us stronger. The most important lesson I learned from my mother was how not to raise my children. I vowed to be a better mother to my little ones than she was to me. I have been blessed with patience, played an active role in my children's lives, told them from the day they were born until the day I could no longer speak that I loved them and hugged them often. I refrained from criticism as much as possible, encouraged when necessary, and proudly complimented their accomplishments until their faces beamed with pride. I hope they would remember me as a good and loving mother.

Standing next to her bed, I stared down at her peaceful body. I watched her chest rise and fall with each rhythmic breath as she lay alone in the queen size bed. Out of all of the people in this world, how did I end up with her as a parent? The question made me stop and think about what my guide had previously mentioned. *If my children chose me as their parent, did I do the same with my mother?* I turned to my guide.

"Did I choose her as my parent before I was born?"

"Yes, as did your children choose you."

"I was supposed to learn something from her?" I assumed.

"Did you?"

Other than being a better parent, what did I learn? I learned gossiping was harmful to others. No matter how much someone tries to influence my decisions, I must stay true to my heart and make choices on my own. I think the most difficult and final lesson I learned was to walk away from drama, even if the person causing it was someone close to me.

Mother rolled toward me and placed her hands under her cheek as if she was praying. Her aged face caused me to reflect further on her life. She had juggled working fulltime while maintaining a neat and clean household and arranged her work scheduled to accommodate my after-school sports. Much of her time in recent years was spent volunteering in church activities.

I imagine my decision to stop communicating with her hurt her feelings quite deeply. She was no longer invited to attend our family holiday gatherings. I did not reply to her occasional message left on my cell phone. As the children became older, they cringed at the mention of her name and came up with excuses when they did not want to spend time with her. The situation was unfortunate. It was as if she had been cheated out of a family, out of being a grandmother. I imagined she would grow old and die alone in the very same bed in which she now lay.

As I reflect on her role in my life, she had remained steadfast and unchanging characteristically. Is that why I chose her as my mother?

"I forgive you, Mom, for all of your transgressions whether intended or not. You are who you are for a reason that has yet to be revealed to me. I just hope I learned what was required so I don't have to endure this experience again."

"*We must continue on.*" My guide urged.

I needed to ensure she had closure.

~

Her phone rang three times before she answered.

"Hello."

The sound of her voice sent a shudder up my spine. I was instantly angry but tried to keep it in check.

"Hello."

"Well, hello you."

"I just wanted you to know that I don't hate you. I just couldn't deal with your gossiping any longer."

"Oh, I don't gossip."

Of course, she would deny it. I wasn't going to argue with her. She saw things in her own way and there wasn't a point in trying to change it.

"I quit talking to you because I couldn't tolerate the drama you created in our family."

"Oh, I know."

Her tone was merry, but flippant as if she was proud. I needed to tell her the one thing she yearned to hear.

"Well, that's all I called to say except... I love you. Good-bye mother."

~

She opened her eyes.

"I love you too. Good-bye." She rolled over and returned to sleep.

I almost laughed out loud, for her response brought to my mind a memory of when I was a little girl. I was congested with a cold and could not find the Vick's. Mom was asleep in bed. Out of frustration I went to her bedroom and asked her where she put it. She sat up in bed, looked at me, and said, "I don't know." I thought her response was rather odd. Mom knew everything, or so she thought. When I asked her about it the next morning, she remembered nothing of our conversation. I wonder if she was awake enough to remember this dream.

With one final glance around the room, I closed my eyes and imagined my next destination.

My Son

I stood at the end of my son's bed. He lay on his stomach sleeping just as he did when he was a baby. I remember with fondness the sleepy-eyed toddler with his arms held upward silently pleading for me to pick him up from his crib. I would snuggle him closely and kiss his warm, blushed cheek as he wrapped his tiny arms around my neck. Oh, how I loved to cuddle with him after he woke from his afternoon nap. Those few moments were so precious. When he became fully awake, he usually asked for his sister, his companion and playmate.

Oh, I miss those days; watching him taking his first steps, losing his first tooth, learning to ride a two-wheeler. I recalled the late nights helping him with school projects; my procrastinator who waited until the last minute to complete a project. Mom to the rescue, but isn't that what moms are for anyway? I couldn't criticize him too much. He received highest honors on his report cards even while participating in multiple sports.

An eager high school sophomore in the fall, he had recently obtained his driving permit and was looking forward to getting behind the wheel. Once he logged additional hours on the road for experience and received his license, he could drive himself to practice, something my husband was sure to appreciate.

"Hello, Thomas." I petted the faithful ghostly feline curled near my son's feet, which nearly touched the footboard of his bed.

My, you have gotten so big. He had experienced another growth spurt recently resulting in the purchase of the next shoe and pants size, the third time this year. Nearly as tall as my husband, I'm certain his coaches are pleased to see his growth. Over time he would mature and fill out his gangly body.

Like his father, his personality was easy going. Some may even describe him as laid back. However, he played sports with enthusiasm, which made him a natural leader. Above all, he possessed a kind and compassionate heart. Much like my daughter, he also had gumption. With his natural sense of the business world, I imagined he would prosper in a career as an entrepreneur or work in the field of finance.

Two summers ago, he began a lawn service business. He has two employees, who are his closest friends. From what I have seen, he treats them fairly. After gasoline expenses are paid, each of them receives a percentage of the profits. He provides a cooler filled with bottled water to keep them hydrated on hot summer days. Managing his money wisely, he packs his lunch and snacks each day. I was impressed by his wise and somewhat conservative business decisions. He truly believed in Ben Franklin's philosophy, 'take care of the pennies and the dollars take care of themselves.'

It made me sad to think I would no longer be in the stands when he played in a game or competed. Most recently, he made the varsity high school baseball team as a freshman, quite an accomplishment. Even though I was very ill, I attended nearly every baseball game. It was time well spent and I believe appreciated, but on the cool spring days, it chilled me to my bones. Many of those days I was bundled in blankets on the bleachers or watched from the comfort of the car.

I prayed he would remember me as a supportive parent, understand the pride that swelled within my heart for his achievements and the person he was becoming, and hoped my eternal love was enough to last him a lifetime. However, until he had children of his own, he probably wouldn't understand the emotions I experienced as a proud parent.

I stepped to the side of the bed and smiled at his handsome face. I focused on what I wanted him to know.

~

I came down the stairs to our basement, or as it was called, 'the man cave.' It had been a project my husband and son had taken on together. They had spent hours painting, staining, and constructing a bathroom, bedroom, and bar area in our walkout basement that faced the lake. It was tastefully done and decorated with a sports theme. I peeked over the wooden railing to see my son sitting at the granite topped bar. He looked as if he had just finished mowing lawns.

I appeared on the couch opposite the bar. His back was toward me. He popped a can of soda open, inclined his head, and drank nearly half of it before rotating his barstool to face me. A curious expression, perhaps one of disbelief, masked his face. I floated to the recliner chair on the other side of the room, which was butted against the picture window and sat. It had been a gift from my family, a very kind gift toward the end of my life. The electric seat would rise to support my weakened legs until I stood firmly on the floor. The massaging back also helped to ease my pain. When I was alone, I would rotate the chair toward the lake and watch its activity. The rippling of the water, geese and ducks paddling about with their young, and people in their boats or on their jet skies were the usual entertainment.

My son stared, realizing that I was no longer sickly and emaciated. I was the person I wished him to remember, healthy and vibrant.

The large picture window behind me framed the cloudless sky and deep blue lake.

My eyes twinkled with pride, and I smiled. I tried to sound lighthearted and not too sentimental.

"I love you."

"I love you too, Mom."

"Buy properties." I knew he was searching for a solid investment for his money he had earned through his small business. It was the best advice I could give him.

"I will."

"Good-bye."

~

He woke, noted the time on his alarm clock, rolled over, and went back to sleep.

My guide came to the foot of the bed.

"*He will remember your dream.*"

I smiled, knowing he would be fine. Oh, there would be days when he would miss me, but he would be fine.

Day 3

My Time Draws Near

I looked at my son's bedroom window. The sun was beginning to peek above the horizon. I needed to visit my daughter and husband one last time. I turned to my guide.

"When must I cross over?"

"*Your life expired at 11:17am. You shall cross over at that time.*"

"With my funeral Mass beginning at 11:00, I will miss most of it." My chin lowered toward my chest.

Wanting to spare my family from second guessing what I would have wanted, I prearranged the music, readings, and designed the little pamphlets each guest would receive before being seated. Like the director of a play, I wanted to see the performance, the last thing I created in my lifetime, but I would miss it. I sighed knowing it was out of my hands. I lifted my chin and glanced toward my guide.

"There's no use in getting upset about something I can't change. At least I can rest assured that I did my best to ease my family's burden."

Before leaving my son's room, I noted the sky had turned to a brilliant spectrum of yellow, orange, pink, and blue morning light.

I went to my daughter's room to say good-bye.

My Daughter

Her angelic face lay peacefully upon her pillow. I knew today would be difficult for her but was thankful to see she was able to sleep and escape the impending sadness of the funeral for a few more moments.

It plagued me to know I would be physically absent from her high school graduation, sending her off to college, celebrating her first real job, waiting at the end of the aisle as I watched her father walk her toward her future husband on her wedding day, and cuddling her children. My anguished heart seemed to shrink in size knowing I would be absent during these and other milestones in her life. I exhaled a cleansing breath in an attempt to ease my disappointment.

You are amazing. I was tempted to brush the lock of blonde hair from her cheek and tuck it behind her ear.

She possessed such spirit, drive, and passion for life. When she was young, it was easy to recognize her determination to succeed at whatever she set her mind to accomplish. Secretly I prayed she wouldn't get hurt during a daring athletic attempt, but I knew I had to remain silent and let her try. My job was to pick her up after the fall and encourage her to keep trying.

Peer pressure and fitting in at school was a challenge for her, especially during the awkward junior high school years. At that age, children are experiencing physical and hormonal changes beyond their control. They may appear like young adults, but they lack the emotional skill and maturity to handle the responsibility. Having a boyfriend was all the rage, as well as the latest fashion. My daughter didn't experience a boy craziness faze, but her passion for clothing and shoes had to be kept in check.

We established a budget and agreed to spend one afternoon a month shopping at the mall, contingent on her sports schedule. With running a business, I had more pressing issues to handle than shopping. In truth, I hated shopping and felt it was a waste of my time. I had to psych myself up, force myself to relax, and enjoy the day. Now that I look back, it was time well spent, just the two of us. We would often eat lunch, visit nearly every store, and do some people watching while we enjoyed a scoop of our favorite flavor of ice cream. It was almost comical to walk with her and watch the eyes of the young men as we passed by them. Some would stare in her direction while others would check out her backside once they passed by her. I don't blame them. I stared at her beautiful face. *Simply stunning.*

I watched her sleep, just as I did when she was an infant. The rise and fall of her abdomen and rhythmic breathing was peaceful.

I tried to think of what I wanted to tell her. I didn't want to sound too cliché. We had many talks over the years; boys, drugs, drinking, friends, high school drama, and her goals for the future. I think we said about all that needed to be said.

My guide came near me.

"*Tell her not to be afraid today. She will understand.*"

I looked at the sincere expression upon his face.

"She will understand?" I paused in contemplation. "I don't understand. What is going to happen today that could make her feel afraid?"

"*It is not your concern, but your message will give her the reassurance that all is well and as it should be.*"

I nodded in agreement. Apparently, I was going to be kept in the dark.

"Very well, but wait, is there something I should be afraid of?"

"*No.*"

With my guide's reassurance, I looked at my daughter. Over the years friends and family would comment on our likeness, but they were wrong. She was more beautiful both inside and out. It was true that she looked like me, but she possessed my husband's self-confidence and motivation. I knew she would be successful in which ever endeavor or pathway she chose in life.

I focused on my intended message.

~

A beautiful melody was playing from the living room as I washed the dishes at the kitchen sink. I wiped my hands on a dish towel and stood silently in the doorway as I watched her hands dance over the ivory keys. At the completion of the song, I applauded.

"Well done."

She rotated the stool to face me.

Crossing the room, I stopped before her.

"Oh, I didn't know you were listening."

"I just wanted to tell you that I love you very much. I am so proud of the person you have become." I brushed back her long blonde hair and tucked it over her shoulder. "Whatever happens today at the funeral, don't be afraid." I relayed my guide's advice.

"What should I fear?" Her face registered concern.

"I don't know, nothing I guess." I admitted.

She stared at me as if questioning my motive, but then smiled.

"Well, I have kept you from your practicing long enough. I must finish the dishes." I watched her rotate the stool toward the keyboard, search through the sheet music, and begin to play. I went back to the kitchen but looked over my shoulder at her one final time.

~

She threw back the covers and sat on the edge of her mattress for a moment. Brushing her hair away from her face, she yawned before heading to the bathroom. When she returned, she got back into bed and pulled the covers over her. Apparently, she wasn't ready to begin the day.

I needed to say one last good-bye.

My Husband

Standing at his bedside, he seemed so alone lying there by himself. My heart ached knowing he would go on without me, yet I wanted the remainder of his life to be happy. If the opportunity should present itself, I hoped he would fall in love again. He was a wonderful man who should grow old in the company of another. Even though the children were with him now, eventually they would leave to begin their lives wherever their career or spouse may take them.

Spooky lay curled at his feet asleep. At least he had the cat to keep him company for a few more years. Maybe he would get another cat, or perhaps a dog. He had always wanted a dog, but I convinced him early on in our marriage that a cat was a more practical pet. They were easier to take care of and a better fit for our busy lifestyle.

Floating above the bed horizontally, I laid gently next to him, hoping not to disturb his sleep. Daring to snuggle as closely as possible, I studied each feature of his face; his strong chin, prominent nose, closed eyes, and eyebrows that seemed to grow bushier with age. I hoped the image of his face would always remain etched within my memory.

I wondered if he was relieved that my fight was over or if he missed the chaos of juggling the children's schedules and spending time with me at the hospital. I placed my palm against his cheek, ran my finger over his soft lips, and wished I could calm his disheveled charcoal hair.

The first year after my passing would be the most difficult; birthdays, our anniversary, holidays, and family vacations. Planning family events and gifts had been my responsibility, but as my illness progressed, it became more difficult for me to do. At my request, we discussed each gift, and he would do the shopping. It was a way of grooming him for the transition.

The loss of a loved one is never easy. Time doesn't heal the heartache. It only dulls it. I believe my husband will always hold a place within his heart for me, as I will forever hold a place within my heart for him.

He mumbled in his sleep as he often did, rolled onto his side away from me, and began to snore. At least he wouldn't have me poking him in the ribs anymore.

I rose and went to the other side of the bed. His arm hung over the edge of the mattress. I traced my finger down his left arm to his wedding ring. I assumed he would continue to wear it, at least for a while.

I watched him sleep until daylight brightened the sky. I looked at my guide knowing my time was drawing to a close.

He nodded as he read my thought.

Spooky stood, arched his back, and stretched his legs. He looked at his sleeping master with one thing on his mind - breakfast. The alarm clock with a heartbeat tiptoed cautiously to my husband's face and brushed his whiskers against his cheek.

Raising his arm subconsciously, he pulled the cat toward his chest before returning to sleep. He had learned long ago to keep his eyes closed and pretend he was sleeping. The tactical stall could sometimes fool Spooky, but not always. This time, however, I was quite certain my husband was sincerely asleep.

I smiled at the two of them. They were such a pair. As a child, my husband's family only had dogs. He was not thrilled about the idea of us having a cat for a pet. At first, he didn't know how to interact with them. He even set one of our first kittens onto the floor quickly and turned to me.

"What's wrong with it?"

I picked it up and listened.

"It's purring because it's happy." I had to suppress my laughter.

Over the years, he had grown quite fond of our cats and treated them as if they were one of our children.

Before Spooky stirred to wake him, I focused on my message and concentrated.

~

He lay asleep with Spooky curled within his arms as if holding a precious child dearly. Their heads rested against the steering wheel in the cab of a red pickup truck. It was parked in the lot of Home Depot, one of my husband's favorite places to shop.

The passenger door window was frosted much like a glass shower door for privacy. It represented the barrier between his physical world and mine. Pressing my forehead and the palm of my hands with my fingers spread wide against the glass, I waited.

He opened his eyes and stared at the passenger window. It took a moment for him to comprehend the fuzzy, gray shadow of someone on the other side, but was uncertain who it could be.

Maintaining my shadowed appearance, I passed through the window and leaned toward his face.

"I might have to go home." I kissed him on his forehead. "I love you." I left the cab of the truck.

~

I watched as he reached for his forehead and touched the spot I had kissed. I wondered if he had felt it.

"I might have to go home." He whispered. "Might? How do you might anything?"

Realizing his master had awakened, Spooky jumped down from the bed, held his fluffy tail high as he turned in circles, and meowed.

My husband sighed as he glanced at the cat, perhaps reluctant to get out of bed. He looked at the ceiling, transfixed on nothing in particular. I assumed he was replaying the dream in his mind and hoped he picked up on my key word.

"Might." He smiled. "Honey, you always used the word 'might' when you had to travel for business."

It was true. It was difficult for me to leave my family. In a way, the word 'might' made my impending departure less certain, but unavoidable.

My conscious was eased knowing he had understood the dream.

A slight smile appeared on his face.

"I love you too, honey." He was prodded by Spooky's impatient meowing. "Yes, yes, I'm coming." He pushed back the blankets, swung his feet to the floor, and sat up.

Spooky meowed again.

"A little patience would be appreciated." He warned the cat as he went into the bathroom and closed the door.

I turned to my guide.

"I knew he would make the connection. I used to tell him 'I might have to go' somewhere before I traveled for business." I explained.

It had been a while since I traveled, but I was certain if he mentioned the dream to the children, they would recall me saying the expression and reaffirm the dream was a message from me.

Spooky pawed at the bathroom door until it opened.

"Yes, I'm coming." My husband assured as the feline rushed toward the stairway. As if to ensure his meal ticket was following, Spooky stopped descending every few steps, which caused my husband to nearly trip several times.

Not Just Another Morning

My family's morning routine commenced as usual, except for the fact that I was dead. After feeding the cat, my husband made coffee. The crunch of each spoonful of cereal resonated as the children ate silently. I assumed the funeral was weighing heavily upon their minds. No one welcomes a final good-bye to a parent, spouse, or even worse, a child. However, it is an emotional task the living may be obligated to face.

Thomas brushed against my leg to draw my attention. Reaching down, I stroked his fur once before he scampered off to sit on the floor beside my son's chair. His beady little eyes looked upward and his tongue licked his lips in anticipation.

My son, as usual, was ravenous. He finished one large bowl of cereal and poured a second. My husband, the toast maker, had set a saucer stacked with several slices upon the table and opted for his usual two cups of coffee with cream and sugar and toast on the side. My daughter ate a small bowl of granola while nibbling on a piece of toast she topped with jelly.

"What should I wear?" My daughter looked at my husband for his advice. He paused with a slice of toast part way to his mouth.

"The two of you often shopped. Did she have a favorite outfit you purchased?"

"Not that I know of."

"Then choose something in her favorite color." Glancing at his watch, it was eight o'clock. "We have to leave soon, so whatever you feel is best will be fine." He reassured before finishing a slice of toast, washing it down with a sip from his mug, and selecting a second from the stack.

Spooky stepped onto the rung of the chair, tapped my son's thigh with his paw, and pleaded for the remaining milk in his bowl. *Moocher*. As usually, my kindhearted son shoveled the last spoonful of cereal into his mouth and gave into the cat's demands. He set his bowl upon the floor before putting his spoon in the dishwasher and leaving the room. Spooky lapped up the contents of the bowl. Curious, Thomas stuck his nose into the bowl as well.

Would Thomas remain like an invisible shadow at my son's side throughout his life and greet him in the afterlife? Perhaps. I prayed for the faithful cat, who yearned for his master's affection.

My daughter put her empty dishes in the dishwasher and went to her room to dress. I assumed she would base her choice of attire on what she thought would please me most. I hoped she wouldn't struggle over the decision too much. It didn't really matter what she chose to wear.

Now alone, my husband popped the last bite of toasted crust into his mouth and cherished a moment of solitude and quiet. I wondered what he was thinking as he watched the birds eating from the birdfeeder outside the kitchen window.

A bright red cardinal landed on the top of the birdfeeder and stared at my husband.

"That's strange. We usually see cardinals only in the winter." I turned to my guide. He was smiling.

"*It is a symbol many associate with their loved ones. Is it not one of your favorite birds?*"

"It is, that and bluebirds."

My husband watched the bird tilt its head to the right and left as if analyzing him. Glancing at his watch again, he tipped his mug upward drinking the last of his coffee before picking up the bowl from the floor, tidying the kitchen, and going upstairs to shower and dress.

Their agenda for the day would involve greeting guests at the funeral home, saying their good-byes in private before my casket was closed, and going to the church for the funeral Mass. Afterward, they would follow my casket to the cemetery, and watch as it was lowered into the ground before returning to the church for a late lunch sponsored by church volunteers. It would be an emotional day filled with reassurances from others, tears, and, I hope, a few smiles.

I entered the bedroom as my husband stepped into the bathroom and closed the door. Within moments I heard water filling the sink. *Shaving before his shower.*

Atop of my dresser was a small box containing costume jewelry. I wasn't one to spend a lot of money on trinkets, but I had acquired several pieces I cherished and wore often. Many were gifts from friends.

I labored over the writing of my will and avoided it for as long as possible. In my mind, writing it was an acknowledgement of my eminent death. But isn't it a fate that awaits us all? I had taken an inventory of my worldly possessions. It was a short list and enabled my final wishes to be written with ease.

I stepped to the window to view my flower garden below. It was not as I remembered.

When we first moved into our home, I decided to tame the area of the lawn on the south side of the house into a place of beauty. Tearing out grass and a few stray bushes, I outlined several planting areas with melon sized rocks. Flat stones were used to create a twelve-foot diameter circle in the center that served as a patio, and mulched pathways were woven between the planting areas and ended at the circle's edge. My husband built an arbor and picket fence that could be seen from the road.

I adorned the archway with a honeysuckle plant on each side and flower boxes displayed vibrant annuals along the fence.

The garden began with a few perennials I had purchased. Friends were eager to donate their divided perennials to the garden. In the fall, I planted tulip and daffodil bulbs, but learned all too soon that my tulips wouldn't survive the ravenous appetites of the deer and squirrels. The daffodils with their variety of bright, sunny colors flourished.

A bird house was installed in the center of each planting section and was inhabited by bluebirds or sparrows. Each Spring I placed a white cast iron table and its four chairs on the patio. On warm sunny spring days, I would sit like a statue and drink my morning coffee in the garden while listening to the echoed chirps of the baby birds as their parents arrived with bugs in their beaks for their feeding.

I like to think my garden was inviting. Neighbors and strangers out for a stroll would knock on our door and ask permission to tour it. I assume curiosity got the better of them. As a good host, I usually accompanied them through the gate in the arbor and answered any questions they may have. After putting in the work and maintaining the garden's beauty, it was nice to have others appreciate my labor of love.

I cringed. It didn't look like that any longer. Weeds had crept into the beds. Windswept seeds had taken root and prospered in the pathways. My countless hours of grooming had been overthrown by nature. I wondered if my husband would hire a landscape company to maintain the garden. Maybe my kind neighbor would come over from time to time while my husband was at work and attempt to keep it in order. If it became unmanageable, I assumed it would be removed and reseeded with grass. Its fate was no longer my concern. I enjoyed it while I was alive. It was a way for me to decompress from my hectic daily schedule, my therapy time, and gave me a sense of accomplishment by creating something for myself, my family, and others to enjoy.

The door opened to the bathroom. *He is the fastest shower taker I know.* I watched him emerge dressed only in his underwear, go to the closet, and punch his legs through his suit pants. He seemed in a hurry.

"Are you two about ready?" He yelled through the closed door of our, his, bedroom as he tucked his dress shirt, zipped and belted, grabbed his suit jacket, and left the room leaving behind the fragrance of his aftershave in his wake.

Leaving My House

I turned and looked out the window as the chaotic scurrying of my family echoed from downstairs.

It was a beautiful day with the sun shining brightly and the dissipating clouds revealing a blue sky. The alarm clock on my nightstand foretold the coming hour. I was a little apprehensive about crossing over. I wondered if it was painful. I snorted. *Silly me. Being dead, I don't know how I can possibly feel any pain.*

My pain, now a memory, had been accompanied by suffering and frustration. I no longer felt its torment, but often wondered why I was subjected to such a prolonged and helpless ending to my life. What moral crime had I committed to be sentenced to such a torturous wrath upon my body or was the method of my death preordained prior to my birth, but for what reason?

Prior to my illness, I lived a happy and fulfilling life. I was blessed to have a loving husband, beautiful children, and a successful career. Maybe I was too attached to this life and the only way I would accept my fate was to endure the pain and suffering which forced me to welcome my death. A pang of guilt wretched my heart, for it was unfair that my family was subjected to my prolonged illness. Was it a lesson they had to learn too?

The moment was soon approaching for my soul to cross over. I turned to my guide for reassurance and confirmation of my assumption.

"Should I be afraid?"

"No. I will remain by your side."

"Good. Is it painful?"

"No."

A dull hum echoed throughout the house as the garage door closed, confirming my family's departure for the funeral home. I began to tour each room one final time.

Spooky was curled like a giant cotton ball upon the seat of a chair in the kitchen sound asleep. After finishing my son's bowl of milk, he took advantage of his vacant warm seat. I petted him before looking to the floor at Thomas. Stroking his fur, I empathized with his loneliness.

"Am I able to take Thomas with me?"

"It is not allowed."

"Why hasn't he crossed over?"

"*I am uninformed of his purpose but assume he may be watching over someone.*"

Since Thomas appeared to be attached to my son, it was a valid assumption.

Entering the living room, I went to my desk and sat in the chair.

"It's a shame that my family was unaware of me being near them after I died." I looked at my guide hovering in the doorway.

"*Many leave an object or appear as their favorite animal, bird, or insect. It is a symbol of their presence. Unfortunately, it may not be recognized as such.*"

"A symbol?"

"*Yes, they appear near their loved one as a bird or dragonfly. Some leave a coin or a feather.*"

A symbol. I contemplated an object, one that would be understood by my family. I wasn't one to throw money around. I was mindful of every penny I earned, so dropping a coin here or there would be uncharacteristic of my former life. If I chose the symbol of a bird, dragonfly, or any other creature of nature, would they simply overlook it? It needed to be something I could place in their pathway where I was certain they would see it yet realize it should not be where they found it. I thought about the birds in my flower garden and those that ate at the bird feeder outside of the kitchen window.

"A feather would be nice." I decided as I rose and traced my fingertips across the glass on the top of my desk. Maybe they would associate it with the wings of an angel. "Could I leave one here?"

My guide reached into a fold in his robe, extracted a white feather, and handed it to me. I rotated it between my fingers examining its structure.

"I never took the time to admire a feather's beauty before." It was light and silky soft with all of its delicate barbs perfectly pointing toward the tip. The wispy down near the quill reminded me of a cloud. I placed the feather on the top of my desk, hoping the cat would not disturb it before it was discovered.

I took one last look around the room before closing my eyes and pictured my final earthly destination.

The Funeral Home

Dark circles underlined my husband's eyes. He ran his hand through his hair as he turned toward another visitor requesting a moment of his time and forced a grateful smile upon his face. People had come to pay their respects and view my body before my casket was closed.

My daughter was standing with some friends watching the video about my life. She had decided to wear the navy floral print dress we had purchased together while shopping one day at the mall. It was a simple dress but complimented her in every way. I watched as she pointed and smiled at the video before explaining the picture to her friends.

I chuckled as I watched my son endure a sympathetic hug from a rather overly endowed woman I did not know. I assumed she was the wife of the man who was shaking hands with my husband, probably a business associate. The woman looked a lot younger than the gentleman. A second marriage perhaps? Either way, my son's face flamed red with embarrassment. He tried to resist the temptation of staring at her chest. Being a normal teenage boy, he glanced around the room to see if anyone was watching him before nonchalantly peeking from the corner of his eye at her bosom.

Gliding around the room and weaving my way between the many visitors, I overheard conversations here and there. I discovered their topic of discussion was similar to yesterday. What can one really say? It would be disrespectful to mention derogatory things about the deceased even if they were a terrible person. However, if the deceased was a terrible person, it may have been their purpose to teach others to live their lives much differently than they had done so.

Stepping into the hallway, I noticed the funeral home director emerging from an adjoining visitation room. The name of the person lying in rest was displayed on a sign by the doorway. It was unfamiliar to me. I peeked into the room to see rows of empty chairs and only one gentleman sitting before the casket, a priest. The room was vacant of flowers. Entering the small room, I stopped halfway down the aisle between the rows of chairs.

"What day is it?"

"*Saturday.*"

It was strange to see the room so empty. Maybe the visiting hours were later in the afternoon, but on a Saturday. It made little sense.

"I don't understand. Where is everyone?"

"I'm right here." An unfamiliar voice replied from behind me.

I turned around to see an elderly man in ragged, outdated clothes leaning against the wall next to the doorway. His scraggly white beard and hair hung well past his shoulders. He held his arthritic hand outstretched toward me as he stepped forward.

"I'm Old Bill. It's a pleasure to meet you." The crow's feet at the corner of his sapphire eyes enhanced his kind smile.

"The pleasure is mine." I clasped his hand within mine.

I looked at the casket. It was an inexpensive model. The face of the deceased within it was clean shaven and its body dressed in a new suit.

"Is that ..." I began as I pointed to the open casket.

"Yep, that's me. I clean up pretty good, don't I?" He stated proudly and smiled.

I couldn't help but notice his teeth were gapped like the spaces between the slats of a picket fence.

"You're quite handsome." I complimented. "If you don't mind me asking, where are your guests?"

"Oh, I don't have any, except for the priest." Old Bill nodded his head in the direction of his only guest. "He found me on the street one day, me and my dog, Brutus. Now where is that darn dog?" He scanned the room in search of his loyal friend.

Upon hearing his name, the chestnut bloodhound popped his head out from behind the casket.

"There you are you old dog. Come here."

The hound's long, droopy ears flopped back and forth as he trotted down the aisle. He sat obediently next to Old Bill, who patted his head before continuing with his story.

"The priest would give us a few sandwiches, a cup of coffee, and visit for a little while. We would see him maybe once a week and surely appreciated his company. It's mighty lonely living on the streets." He admitted as if he still felt the emptiness of his former life. He pulled his shoulders back, straightened a bit taller, and forced a smile.

"Now that you're here, I guess I can count you as a guest, so that makes two."

"Yes, that makes two guests." I smiled.

He was genuinely sincere and humble. It was a pity our lives had not crossed while we were both alive.

As whispered conversations echoed down the hallway from my crowded viewing room, I realized how my life had been enriched by friends and family. I pictured him walking the streets or sitting on a park bench, ignored, and shunned by society, and cuddling with Brutus for warmth as they slept wrapped in a blanket on a cold winter night.

"If you want to know, just ask. I don't bite." Old Bill chuckled to break the silence.

"I'm sorry. I didn't mean to be rude." I looked at Brutus momentarily before staring at Old Bill's eyes once again. "I was just curious about your life. Why were you homeless?"

"I served honorably in the war but prefer not to talk about it. I missed the unity of the men I served with and once arriving home, that unity disappeared. I guess I never adjusted to everyone living separately in society."

"Separately?"

"Yes, separately. When I served, we did everything together, close knit, and supported each other. Once home, those of us who survived went our separate ways. It was like losing a family and I was the only one left."

"What about your family? Friends?"

"They didn't understand what I was going through, so I left them and did the best I could on my own. Oh, I held down a job or two here and there, but after a while I withdrew from society.

"You must have lived an interesting life."

"Some may think so. My life on the street was one of solitude." His line of vision rested upon Brutus. "I remember the day I found a dirty little pup. He was thrown out by someone, homeless just like me. I did my best to clean him up, nurse his scrapes and scratches, and fed him what I could scrounge up. He grew quickly."

Old Bill petted the dog affectionately.

"He would watch over me while I slept, kept me safe. On many days, he was my only company. Oh, I would bump into a friend or two now and then, but I knew Brutus would always be by my side through thick and thin. He got sick one cold winter and died in my arms, but he was waiting for me, kind of appeared as I took my last breath. I guess he was always there next to me even though I couldn't see him."

I turned toward my guide behind me. I didn't want to be rude, so I posed the question in my mind.

Where is his guide?

My spirit guide looked toward the ceiling. I followed his line of sight to see the guide floating above.

"I know, that dang spook keeps following me everywhere I go." Old Bill glanced over his shoulder.

"He isn't a spook. He is a guide."

"A guide to what?"

"To help you cross over."

"Cross over to where?"

"I don't know, but I assume Heaven."

"Heaven? Oh, I don't know if I am worthy. I killed a lot of men in the war."

"I believe everyone is worthy." I stated what my heart truly felt. I wasn't quite certain what Old Bill's purpose was, but I think his later years taught others compassion, or at least one person. I looked at his only guest.

Old Bill combed his long gray beard with his fingers while he thought.

"Wherever I go from here, I hope Brutus can come with me."

His guide descended to the floor. He nodded his head in affirmation.

"He will always be by your side." I patted Brutus on the head and smiled at Old Bill. "Trust your guide."

My husband's voice echoed from the hallway.

"We will meet you at the church." He reaffirmed to one of the departing guests.

"I need to get back to my family. It was good to meet you Old Bill."

He clasped my extended hand between his weathered, wrinkled palms.

"The pleasure was mine."

Stepping into the hallway, I looked over my shoulder to see my new friend staring at me. I waved farewell. He lifted his hand in a silent reply.

Spirits I had met since my death were not accompanied by a guide, yet Old Bill was, and I could see him. Why couldn't I see the spirit guides for my family and others? A curious thought caused me to ask my guide for an explanation.

"Everyone has a spirit guide, right?"

"*Yes, and sometimes more than one.*"

"So why am I able to see Old Bill's guide and not the ones watching over my husband and children?"

"*Were you able to see me when you were alive?*"

"No."

"*As you are unable to now.*"

"I don't understand."

"*You are watching your family like an outsider looking in. You cannot see their spirit guides as they cannot see them. They are in the nonphysical world, a different dimension.*"

"So, their guides are in the physical dimension, but remain invisible." I believe I understood.

My guided nodded in confirmation.

The funeral director and his assistant waited patiently inside the doorway as the last guest shook my husband's hand and left the room. The double doors closed behind me allowing my family the privacy for their final good-bye. As instructed, the ushers waited in the hallway for their queue.

The tall red sconces with their protective flickering flames would soon be snuffed out. They were no longer needed to watch over the vessel for my soul. I stared down at my expressionless face. Gone were the emotions of joy, sadness, and pride. I had taken them with me. There was only emptiness, yet unbeknownst to my family and friends, I continued to live on.

I looked at my family as they approached my casket. Their arms were wrapped around each other's waists as if they were holding each other up.

"Good-bye Mom. I hope you are at peace and with the angels in Heaven. I will miss you." My son's bottom lip quivered.

"I will miss you too, sweetheart." I placed the palm of my hand against his cheek.

"Bye, Mom. I love you. I'm glad you are no longer in pain. I miss you too. It won't be the same without you. But rest assured, you will always be in my heart." My daughter dabbed tears from her cheeks with a facial tissue.

"I love you too." I kissed the damp line on her cheek.

"Good-bye. You know I love you. I will not forget all that we discussed and promise to do my best." My husband sighed.

"I love you, dear, with all of my heart." I watched him grasp the top of the casket above my head.

Don't forget the jewelry.

He looked at my peaceful face one last time and hesitated. Releasing his grasp, he removed the necklace, bracelet, rosary, and rings from my body. He dropped them into the inside pocket of his suit coat.

Thank goodness you remembered. Good job, honey.

My son glanced about the room as if looking for something.

"Where are the flowers, Dad?"

"Most were taken to the gravesite. A few of them are at the church." My husband lowered the casket lid.

The funeral director and assistant came forward silently, inserted a key in each lock, and turned them until a click resonated within the room. I thought of the many times I had turned a key within a lock, the countless times I had locked our house to keep everything within it secure. It was a simple act, but now the turn of a key enclosed my body safely for eternity.

My family watched numbly as the director centered a bouquet of pale pink roses on the casket lid like a bow on a present. The assistant opened the doors and allowed the pallbearers, nicely dressed in their suits, to enter the room in a single line. With the guidance of the funeral director, they took their assigned place around the casket, escorted it out of the room, and into the back of a white hearse. Why white? I wanted the color that enclosed my body to represent the love and light shining down from Heaven instead of having it surrounded by the deathly darkness of a black hearse. I had requested a powder blue limousine, the color of the sky, to chauffer my family for the day. Perhaps my requests were a little quirky, but I preferred to symbolize the end of my life in a positive way.

With headlights twinkling and little orange flags waving on the roofs of the vehicles, my body led the procession with my family and a long line of cars following the short distance to the church.

My Funeral Mass

The solemn parade came to a stop adjacent to the church. The pallbearers took their place at the rear of the hearse while my family emerged from their car and waited patiently. The funeral director swung open the back door, guided my casket out, and into the awaiting hands of the men until the bier's wheels touched the ground. They rolled it through the doorway of the vestibule and stood silently uncertain of what to do next. The funeral director pointed to an alcove where my casket was placed temporarily.

I accompanied my family as they entered the church and stood next to my casket while guests emerged from their vehicles and began to gather inside. The priest greeted my husband and children and expressed his condolence as four altar boys carrying flickering candles, holy water and incense, the bible, and a tall wooden handled crucifix stood behind him awaiting their queue. Not a word was spoken as the priest raised his arms over my casket and his lips moved silently in prayer. Lowering his arms, he pressed his palms together at his chest, bowed his head, and whispered, "Amen." He checked the time on his watch before looking toward my husband.

"We shall begin in a few minutes." He reassured before exiting the area.

Turning away, I stepped inside the nave with its many pews and stained-glass windows illuminated by the natural light from the sun. The intricate pieces of colored glass depicted inspirational moments in Jesus' life, healing the sick, raising the dead to life, the last supper, and his ascension into Heaven. Smaller windows contained colorful portraits of the apostles. An iron candelabrum with its multiple swaying flames was placed on each side of the dais and anchored by a vase of pale pink roses.

My eyes were drawn above the altar to the large cross with Jesus on the wall. Within the hour I would be meeting him soon, or at least I hoped I would be.

Whispered conversations and footsteps on the polished floor echoed from the back of the church. Glancing over my shoulder, I saw several ushers greeting guests, handing them pamphlets, and directing them down the aisle toward empty seats. Once seated, they busied themselves by glancing over the pamphlet, kneeling in prayer, or staring blankly at the altar. I must have done something right during my life for so many friends, business associates, and acquaintances to take the time from their busy schedules to say good-bye.

I looked back to the cross with Jesus staring down at the congregation.

"I don't remember Him."

"*You will.*"

"I always liked attending mass. There was just something about arriving early, the church echoing in quietness, alone with my thoughts, and watching familiar faces take their usual places in the pews. Perhaps it was the sense of community, of belonging to something bigger than myself that I enjoyed. Now that I look back, I wasn't involved in church activities. I was too busy with the children, my business, and life in general, or let me clarify, they were my priority. I should have served on a committee or two and interacted more with members of my church. It was something I intended to do once I retired, a way of staying socially active, and for a good cause."

As usual, my guide was listening, but remained silent.

I watched the guests continue to seat themselves. Again, there were a few unfamiliar faces. I chuckled as a funny thought crossed my mind. It would be creepy to think a stranger attended a funeral out of curiosity. I imagine if someone was bold enough to do so, no one would question the stranger's intent.

I saw my mother enter the church. She glanced toward the alcove at my casket and family before turning into the aisle and walking toward the altar. I reserved a seat for her in the second row behind my family. Standing at the end of the aisle was an usher, who stepped forward and put his hand on the end of the pew indicating her seat. She smiled at his kind face, genuflected, and sat in the pew. Even though she is technically family, I appreciated her keeping her distance from my husband and children. I was thankful she wasn't bold enough to make a scene and sit in the front pew reserved for them. She sat alone with her head cast downward and her shoulders rounded as she pulled her rosary from her purse and began to pray. I wondered if she was praying for my soul or any regrets she may have. She appeared genuinely sad.

I imagine the loss of a child, whether you have a close relationship with them or not, is difficult. As she began to pray, a twinge of compassion pulled at my heart.

My crash course into parenthood was the day my daughter was born. As I held her within my arms and looked into her newborn face, a burden of worry settled upon my shoulders and fear took permanent residence within a portion of my brain. I prayed to be spared the pain and heartache from the death of either of my children. Thankfully, my request was honored.

In her case, my early death seemed to go against the order of nature. Maybe similar thoughts were running through my mother's mind. Was she now experiencing the grief that I was spared? Unfortunately, she had to come to terms and accept my death. Like everyone else in attendance, she needed to say good-bye. Whatever turmoil was between us, I hoped she had understood my message, gathered strength from happy memories, and move forward with her life.

The last of the guests trickled into the nave and were seated quickly. The priest, dressed in his white vestments, stood at the doorway, and signaled an usher, who instructed the pallbearers to wheel my casket to the priest with my family following. Once my casket was in place, an usher removed the roses.

Adjusting his portable microphone, the priest explained to the congregation as he blessed the casket with holy water, incense, and covered it with a white pall embroidered with a gold cross. The roses were replaced as Ava Maria began to play on the organ. The altar boy with the crucifix led the way down the aisle, followed by the remainder of the altar boys, the priest, my casket escorted by the pallbearers, and finally, my family.

I went to the front corner of the room next to the Virgin Mary statue to watch the procession. My brother-in-law must have entered without my noticing. He sat next to my mother. I'm certain my husband appreciated his effort to catch a flight and represent his side of the family.

As the music continued to play, the altar boys climbed the single step onto the sanctuary, set their candles, holy water, and incense upon the altar, and placed the cross in its stand. Another set the bible upon the pulpit. Together the quartet stood before their chairs against a wall to the left of the altar. The priest ascended the step, bowed to the crucifix on the wall, turned, and stood in front of his chair facing the congregation. The pallbearers aligned the casket with the front pews before sitting in the reserved first row to the right. My family filed into the front pew to the left, retrieved a hymnal, and joined in the processional hymn.

It was difficult to read my son's emotion. He stood with a stern expression upon his face, staring blankly at nothing in particular. Maybe he was on the brink of tears and eye contact with someone with a sympathetic expression would be more than he could bear. The stigma that 'crying is for babies' was probably weighing heavily upon his mind. He didn't sing. *Tough guy*. I knew in my heart that it was just his normal teenager transition from a boy into a man coming into play.

I watched as my daughter wiped a tear from her cheek while she sang. I knew she would be emotional.

Grandmother was right. Growing old is filled with good-byes. The older one gets, the more good-byes you say to those who pass before you. I hoped my daughter would live a long life even if it meant she would say many good-byes. I imagined this good-bye would be her most difficult. I prayed she would not experience a deeper loss.

As the organ faded to silence, my husband closed and returned the hymnal to the pew cubby and looked at the statue of Mary before redirecting his attention to the priest.

"In the name of the Father, and of the Son, and of the Holy Spirit." The priest began.

"Amen." The congregation made the sign of the cross on their bodies.

I didn't have much time left. I went to my casket and traced my fingers along the pall as I walked its length. I scanned the many faces in the congregation as I continued down the aisle. Their faces were solemn. Some dabbed a facial tissue to their eyes or noses. A few of the guests moved their fingers to the next bead of their rosaries as their lips moved without words spoken. I saw my neighbor and my business partner sitting next to each other.

The pews were filled, and several people stood against the wall at the back of the church to pay their respect or seek closure.

Closure is an interesting term to describe someone coming to terms with the death of a loved one, or even the death of a pet. The process of dying was a little daunting, but easy. I was moving on to something better and leaving behind my illness and pain. No more worrying about paying bills, meeting deadlines, cleaning the house, weeding flower gardens, and dreading the mundane chore of grocery shopping. Would I miss everyone, most definitely, but maybe somehow, I could watch them from afar or be allowed to stay nearby them like a guardian angel. Maybe I would be reborn in order to learn what I had yet to learn and if I was lucky, be reunited with them in my next life. Or maybe I would wait on the other side for them to join me before we went on to our next lives together. Did they have any inclination of what was to follow their death? I know many believe in life after death, but did they understand there were many lives to live in order to learn, teach, and fulfill their purpose? If they didn't, they were in for a grand surprise. In truth, we don't die. Our soul continues on.

I went to my son.

"You are such a handsome young man, kindhearted, and so very special to me." I looked into his aqua, bloodshot eyes that continued to stare blankly. "I am so very proud of you. I wish you all of the joy and happiness throughout your life. I love you, always and forever." I kissed him on his cheek while the priest continued to speak.

I stood before my daughter as a tear welled in her eye and rolled down her cheek. It was too much of a temptation, so I brushed the tear away with the tip of my finger. To my surprise, I was able to do so. I looked at my guide. He smiled and nodded his head as if he was not surprised.

"How did I do that?"

He simply smiled.

My daughter stared at me. Had she felt me brush away her tear? I watched as she touched her cheek.

"And to you, my sweet daughter, you will always be my little girl. I love you so very much." I kissed her on the cheek before moving to my husband.

"My darling husband, I wish you could hear me now more than ever. I know the days ahead may be filled with sorrow but may memories of happier times replace the sadness. I love you with all my heart. Thank you for enriching my life and all you have done for me." I kissed him on the cheek and retreated to the head of my casket to view them one more time.

A pinpoint of twinkling light came from a wooden beam of the vaulted ceiling. It showered down upon me, making a circle of light on the floor. I looked at my guide. He nodded with encouragement as if to say what was happening was normal.

"*It is time for you to cross over. I will follow right behind you, as always.*"

I looked at my family one last time. It was somewhat troubling to leave them behind, to grieve, and not be there to comfort them. Maybe one day they will come across a silly photograph of me, shed a tear or two, and reminisce on the time that we shared. I hoped the memory would replace the portion of emptiness within their hearts.

The enlightened circle on the polished floor drew the attention of my daughter. Puzzled by its source, she followed the sparkling light upward to its origin before retracing it back down to the floor. Clutching my husband's arm, she drew his attention. He leaned his head toward her.

"Dad, look in front of Mom's casket, on the floor."

He glanced where she had indicated but saw nothing. He looked at her for an explanation.

"What?"

"On the floor in front of Mom's casket." She pointed her finger in the direction of the circle of light.

His eyebrows drew together as he looked at the floor, but he saw nothing.

She squeezed his arm again and pointed to the wooden beam in the vaulted ceiling. He looked up to the ceiling, scanned it quickly, but again saw nothing.

She watched intently as the pinpoint of twinkling light vanished.

I was gone.

My daughter looked back to the floor to discover the circle of light had disappeared as well.

"Dad, did you see that?"

"See what?"

"There was light coming from that wooden beam." She lIfted her chin slightly upward. "It made a large circle on the floor in front of Mom's casket. You didn't see it?"

"No."

"I had a dream last night. Mom was in it. She told me not to be afraid today. Do you think she was referring to the beam of light?"

"Maybe. Were you afraid?"

"No." She smiled.

"Good." He smiled as he put his arm around her shoulders and hugged her affectionately.

The Other Side

Death is the ending of a life, or is it a beginning of the next?

In preparation for my death, I researched and read several testimonials discussing the death of a loved one and the after-death experiences of those who returned from the other side. Many of the stories had similar details.

In the closing hours of life, they mentioned someone standing at the foot of their bed. The apparition, usually someone they knew who had passed before them, encouraged them to follow and not be afraid. The visit was interpreted as a sign that their death was near.

For those who returned from the dead, they described a long, dark tunnel with twinkling daylight at the opposite end. They walked toward the brightness and stepped into a room filled with light and love. Some were given the choice between staying in the serenity of the afterlife and returning to complete tasks yet to be fulfilled. Others were not given a choice and returned with a message for a friend or family member.

Now that I am here, it feels like home. It is indeed filled with light, and I was welcomed by the loving arms of Him.

"Hello." A familiar voice greeted from behind me.

As He released me from his embrace, I gazed into his kind blue and green eyes. Encouraged by His gentle smile, I looked toward my guide who would continue to stand by me through my transitional period between this life and the beginning of the next. I turned around to see who had spoken.

"Hello." I greeted the man standing before me.

He was clean shaven, in his early to mid-forties, and quite handsome. He was smiling at me.

"I'm sorry, do I know you?"

"Yes, we have known each other throughout the centuries."

"Centuries, that's a very long time."

"In your most recent life, I met you in the funeral home after you had died." He hinted with a devilish sparkle in his sapphire eyes.

I scrutinized his face trying to recall who he was. I looked at his strong chin, clean-cut brunette hair, and his eyes, his sapphire eyes.

"Old Bill?"

"Ah, you remember. Very good." He smiled.

Brutus stepped out from behind him, sat, and looked toward his master with his tongue hanging out of the side of his mouth. He appeared younger too.

"I see you followed my advice." I glanced to his spirit guide, who stood behind him.

"Best advice I ever received." He smiled and petted the top of Brutus's head.

I couldn't help but notice the change in appearance of Old Bill. He wasn't old.

"You're so young."

"Yes, we all are. Old age is one of the things we leave behind in our past lives. No longer do we suffer, feel pain, or age. Oh, some of us are very old souls, some are very young, but more than anything, we are blessed to be what we are."

I thought of my family and wondered how they were coping.

"Ah, those you have left behind." He had read my mind. "They will move on with their lives. They have purposes yet to fulfill and things to learn or teach before they join us."

"I miss them already and wish I could let them know that I am fine."

"But you can."

"How?"

He looked at my guide as if to obtain approval.

My guide nodded his head.

"You can communicate with them just as you did the three days following your death."

I looked at my guide.

"I can do that from here?"

"Yes, but time is much different here. It has been three earth days since you have arrived home."

Three days? It took three days? Time must be slower or there were a lot more hours in each day.

"You may let them know you are fine or give them a message anytime you wish. However, it is important to allow them to move forward with their lives, so limited visits are ideal. As suggested previously, a symbol left where they will see it is always welcome."

The feather on my desk. I hope they found it.

"So, I can communicate with them through their dreams as before?"

"That is correct. There may also be times when they send you a heartfelt message. You may want to answer them."

"But how will I hear it?"

"As an echo within your mind."

"Is it nighttime there?"

"Yes, but nearly morning."

I thought of my husband. I wanted to let him know I had crossed over safely, but I thought it would be best to give my message to another, someone certain to receive and understand it.

"Since my daughter is a sensitive, I think she would be more receptive to my message. Do you agree?"

"*She is blessed with the gift more than anyone else in your family. She can relay the information to everyone else.*"

As I closed my eyes, a message from Him was pictured within my mind. I understood and focused on my daughter.

~

She was sitting in the comfy chair with her feet upon the ottoman and watching a sports channel with her dad, who lay upon the sofa. A frameless, rectangle mirror appeared on the adjacent wall above my husband's head.

My daughter watched as my hand reached through the mirror and gave my husband four tickets that were shaped like large rectangles with notched corners. Each ticket had a thin white border. He fanned them out like playing cards in his hand. The top ticket was black, the second red, and two remaining tickets were different in color, but undefined. As I retracted my hand, my daughter watched it intently. Our eyes met.

"*Mom.*"

I smiled as I read her thought and was pleased, she recognized me.

My hair was perfectly in place, my favorite lipstick upon my lips, and my clothing looked like a glowing white angora sweater. I looked healthy, a wallet snapshot of me of sorts, but unlike a photograph, I could move.

"*I'm fine and I'm happy.*" I conveyed without moving my lips. She received my message and understood.

I lifted my hand, wiggled my fingers, and scrunched up my shoulders while lowering my head to look her straight in the eye. I knew she would recall my go-to silly photographic mannerisms that had been captured in so many pictures over the years. It was a connection I was certain she would make. As I waved good-bye, her alarm clock sounded, waking her for work.

~

I opened my eyes and looked at my guide.

"*Well done.*"

"She understood my message?"

"*Yes, your words resonated within her mind, as does your love within her heart.*"

"Good." I grinned in relief. "What happens now?"

"*Since you completed your tasks in your past life, you will prepare for your next life.*"

"My next life? Out of curiosity, how many lives have I lived?"

"*Over one hundred, but it is important to know that the lives you have lived are not nearly as important as the emotion you have experienced during those lives. Love, happiness, sorrow, and all other emotions have helped you to learn and teach others. Those emotions are with you today and always."*

From Beyond The Grave

Book Two of An Afterlife Journey

Brenda Hasse

Available 2018

My Mother's Funeral

My attention was drawn to a circle of light that appeared on the church floor in front of my mother's casket. My eyes traced it upward to a wooden beam in the vaulted ceiling. It didn't make any sense. How can a beam of light come through the ceiling? A calmness settled deep within me alleviating any fear. In fact, I found it comforting.

I clutched my dad's arm and told him to look to the light on the floor, but he saw nothing. I pointed to the strange phenomenon coming from the wooden beam, but it disappeared as he looked at where I had pointed.

Even though the past few days had been stressful, I was certain I didn't imagine what I saw. But as self-doubt crept into my mind, I tried to justify it as a result of the grief I was experiencing.

As the congregation replied "Amen," my mind snapped back to the reality of the situation. The priest droned on, everyone went through the routine 'church aerobics,' and we took our leisurely lap to receive communion.

I never liked attending Mass. It was the same old boring service, except for the readings that changed weekly. Of the entire hour and fifteen minutes, I looked forward to watching people pass by my pew on their way to receive communion. I often saw familiar faces and would smile at fellow classmates who returned a slight indication that they had seen me as well.

But today I really didn't want to see anyone. I kept my head down.

With a final blessing from the priest, the Mass ended. We followed Mom's casket out of the church and watched as the pallbearers loaded it into the hearse.

The drive to the cemetery was a short distance. Mom and Dad had side by side plots. I prayed Dad would not join her for many years to come. I know it sounds selfish of me to say so, but I needed him in my life, if for nothing else, stability.

I had a lot of big things coming up, graduation, college, and hopefully someday, marriage. I wanted him there to walk me down the aisle, especially since I would have to do much, if not all, of the planning without much assistance.

I imagined my wedding would be the most difficult milestone in my life to get through without her. I know it was an event we had talked about often. We had exchange ideas, planned the preliminaries, even though it was premature. I didn't even have a boyfriend. Mom always insisted that I focus on myself, and her sound advice still rings within my mind.

"There is plenty of time for you to have a man in your life, later down the road, after high school. At the moment, you need to focus on yourself. This is your time. One day some good-looking guy will stand back and notice the ambition, confidence, and intelligence you possess and admire those attributes. Then you must decide if he is right for you. Sometime men are attracted to such a woman because they are lazy, and they would just as soon have you take care of them. In truth, that type of person is more like a child, and you would be their mother. You want to be selective and not blinded by love. Examine each suitor's attributes and qualities and ask yourself if you can tolerate their personality for a lifetime. Until that time comes, focus on yourself and what you want to accomplish. Once you get married and especially after you have children, you will find yourself at the bottom of your list of priorities, and that's even if you are on the list."

She had gone on to explain that the average age of a guy getting married is twenty-seven years old.

"Do you think a seventeen or eighteen-year-old guy is serious about a relationship?"

She had a point. It seemed as if couples in my class who hooked up before prom soon separated afterward. For those still going steady, I can only assume the same will happen to them if they attend different universities after graduation.

I took her advice to heart and focused on my studies and sports. I made a habit of 'just being friends' with guys who expressed an interest in wanting more than that. In truth, with Mom's illness, I didn't have the time for them.

"Get in the car, honey." Dad held the door as he waited.

I glanced at him before looking to the hearse to verify Mom was safely inside the white hearse.

After seating myself in the backseat of the light blue limo, the orange flags on each side of the hood of the car waved in the breeze as if they were bidding farewell. I was joined by my brother and dad before our car followed the hearse to the cemetery. I turned and looked out the rear window. The parade of cars with their headlights shining brightly and waving orange flags was long. Turning back, no one spoke the short distance before we passed through the ornate archway of the cemetery. The procession came to a halt on the blacktop pathway adjacent to where the readied plot awaited. It had green indoor/outdoor carpeting around the edges of the rectangle hole. A small canopy tent had been erected with chairs overlooking where Mom would be placed.

We waited in the car for several minutes as the guests parked their vehicles and gathered around the site. Mom's casket was taken out of the hearse and carried by the pallbearers to the grave as we followed. The funeral director placed the rose bouquet on the top of the casket before stepping away. He indicated for us to stand in front of our appointed chairs reserved for the family. The priest began speaking. I wasn't in the mood to listen.

Poems were read and white homing pigeons were released. I watched numbly as her casket was lowered into the ground. Dad used a small chrome shovel to take a bit of dirt and drop it onto the casket lid.

We returned to the car and headed back to the church hall. Some of the guests attended the late lunch, others went home.

I'm not certain which church committee was responsible, but the tables were set with tablecloths and flower centerpieces. The food was buffet style and quite delicious. My compliments to the cooks.

I sat with my brother and Dad at our usual coffee and donuts table. It was strange to see Mom's chair empty. Our uncle sat next to Dad. I was quite surprised when Grandma sat at our table. Maybe she thought it was reserved for family.

Dad ate quickly, excused himself, and left to visit guests seated at other tables. Grandma did so as well.

As the afternoon dragged on, it seemed as if no one wanted to leave, which was opposite of my desire. Many paused at our table on their way out of the hall to express their condolences. I really didn't want to talk to anyone, but I forced a smile upon my face and accepted a hug or two.

My brother leaned next to me and spoke for my ears only

"I'm ready to go. How about you?"

"Yes. Now would be nice, but I know we can't go until everyone has left."

The funeral director entered the hall and handed Dad his keys. He had kindly brought our car from the funeral home to the church hall. Dad expressed our gratitude for all he and his staff had done for us over the past few days.

The last of the guests accompanied us out of the hall. After the short drive home, stepping through the threshold of our house seemed strange. I let out a sigh, for it seemed a little emptier even though the scent of Mom's perfume still lingered.

I went to the kitchen, took a cookie from the cookie jar, and entered the living room where Mom's desk sat empty. So many times, I had entered the room to see paperwork piled high on her desk. She would look over the top of her reading glasses and ask what I wanted. I put the remainder of the cookie in my mouth as I stopped before her desk and stared at the white feather lying on top. I picked it up, twirled it between my thumb and index finger. *Strange. Is this a feather from your angel wings, Mom?*

I went to my room to change into something more comfortable and took the feather with me.

Thank you for reading

On The Third Day

Want to stay updated with news about
Brenda Hasse Books?

* Receive the newsletter by joining:
https://brendahassebooks.com/newsletter-sign-up/
* Like the author on Facebook:
Facebook.com/Brenda.Hasse
* Follow the author on Instagram:
Instagram.com/BrendaHasse/

And if you have a moment, please review
On The Third Day at the store where you bought it. Tell
other readers why you enjoyed this book.
Thank you!